MY DRAGON LORD

Broken Souls 1

ALISA WOODS

Cover by BZN Studio

ISBN: 9781689124720

My Dragon Lord (**Broken Souls 1**)

Ember's stumbled into a lair of desperate dragons— and she's just the thing the Lord of the Lair needs.

I really messed this up.

Pinned to the floor by a billionaire playboy, caught stealing files from his computer.

"I'm trying to decide whether to kiss you or lock you up," he says.

"Kiss me, and there will be blood. Not mine, either."

He just smiles. Rich, powerful, probably used to getting anything he wants.

I'm just here to find my sister—I suspect he and his band of playboys have trafficked her and who knows how many others. I'm here for them too. Eventually.

But now I'm shackled to the wall in his dungeon—a literal dungeon in a literal castle tucked in one of the Thousand Islands at the border of Canada.

I really messed this up.

Ember's a hot-shot reporter. Niko's the sexy Lord of the Lair determined to find his soul mate... and he'll do whatever it takes to save his people from extinction.

My Dragon Lord is a steamy new dragon shifter romance that'll heat up the sheets with love and warm your heart with dragonfire.

ONE

Ember

IT'S PATHETICALLY EASY TO GET IN.

The rich pay little attention to the staff. As an award-winning investigative reporter, *paying attention* is like 90% of what I do. The other 10% is remembering to take showers when I'm working a story. So, tracking down the catering company for reclusive billionaire Nikolais Lord's sex parties? *Easy.* Bribing an underpaid single mom to let me take her shift? *Simple.* (And holy shit, Party Central pays their people *nothing.*) The hardest part is not glaring at the thirsty men drooling over the young women in barely-there dresses being paraded around the man's castle.

Yes, an actual *castle.* In upstate New York's Thousand Islands, where it's easy to hide all your sex trafficking. At least, that's what I think Lord is doing here. To be honest, it looks more like an upscale brothel or even just a "party" for the rich and glamorous. The women look a little too healthy. The men are surprisingly young and way too hot to be your average rich guy looking for underage sex. Or *rape,* as I call it. Because that's what it is. And I've been documenting the carnage from traffickers like Lord, if that's what he's doing, for six months now. It's ugly, and it's everywhere. Even—*especially*—in secret high-society getaways like this castle on an island near the Canadian border.

A man in a finely-tailored black silk shirt takes the last canape off my tray. Then he does a double-take and turns back. "Hello, there…" His gaze drops to my nameplate. *Maria Gomez.* His ridiculously handsome face frowns because my super-pale skin is not even close to the warm brown tone you'd expect with that name. My family is 100% French Canadian, except we were all born on this side of the border. *"Maria.* You're new, aren't you?" Hot Boy's eyes are drinking me in, and not just the v-neck cleavage that Maria's black-and-white uniform exposes. He's checking out *my face* like he expects to pick me out of a lineup.

Shit. "Oops! Time for more canapes." I twirl

away with my tray, hustling back to the kitchen. Rich Boys don't pay attention to the staff—*unless they're predators.* I momentarily forgot that part. Everyone here—even if they don't fit the profile of a buyer, which is literally anyone but mostly middle-aged men—is potentially trawling for young flesh to abuse. I fit the bill on that. I'm a conventionally-attractive female who looks a lot younger than her twenty-eight years. The muscle tone from kick-boxing is covered by the uniform, and I left my black belt in Brazilian Jiu-Jitsu at home. That's the kind of thing guys like Rich Boy discover when they make the mistake of touching me.

I drop the hors d'oeuvres tray in the used pile, snag another one off the rack, then pretend to inspect it so I can delay and regroup. I'm on a mission here, and it's not to punish pretty rich boys for their sins—*not yet,* at least. I'm here to find my sister. She's been missing two days, and it's killing me. Cinder holed up in that crappy apartment of hers in the city, but I didn't think... I'd *hoped* she would come out of that horrible depression she'd fallen into. At least tell me what was wrong. I mean, I know what's wrong—I put her in a horrible situa-tion, and things went terrible, fast. It's my fault. I own that. But to shut me out for a week? Then simply disappear? Something's not right, but I can't get anyone to take that seriously—so I'm doing my own investigation. And the last entry in her planner said *Party@Lord's Castle, Thousand Islands.*

So I'm here.

And she has to be, too. Maybe she was picking up the project again—the documentary we were making together about sex trafficking in America. Rumors have circulated about Nikolais Lord's parties for years—everything from orgies to sex trafficking to psychedelic Burning Man style events on his privately-owned castle island. No one seems to know what he really does up here—or is willing to go on the record. Which says *trafficking* to me. Given my soft-hearted, quiet sister wasn't the kind to party in her hometown of New York City, no way she'd travel six hours north to an island just to—

"You going to count those or move them?" the head caterer snaps at me as he strides past, quickly finding someone else to bark at.

I grimace and follow the next server out the swinging door to the main hall. The place is insanely big—three stories high in the hall, which is topped with a stained-glass dome—with couches and at least three fireplaces on the main floor. Sweeping staircases lead up to dozens of rooms along interior balconies that overlook the main floor, almost like a hotel. There are marble and mahogany, crystal and wrought iron everywhere. The place *screams* money, which doesn't mean there's not trafficking—just that the worst of it probably isn't the well-dressed girls on the main floor with the healthy glow in their cheeks. Maybe high-end escorts? Or maybe Lord lures in vulnerable girls with promises of money or fame, gets them behind closed doors, and then they're trafficked from there.

There are a hundred ways girls get trapped by men like him.

I haven't seen him yet among the young men shopping tonight. I did my homework—Nikolais is American, but his ancestors came from the Greek Isles, and he's got that dark, sexy look, like many of the Hot Boys here tonight. He would stand out, but he hasn't been on the floor for the hour I've been serving. Maybe he's already in one of the rooms? Which works for me. I don't need him—I need whatever secrets he's got in his files in his office. Some clue as to whether he's trapped my sister into whatever hidden operation he's running here.

Time to make my move.

I pick my way through the main hall, stopping

to dispense snacks to a couple making sexy eyes at each other, then work toward the stairs. If Cinder came here, she couldn't whip out her camera without raising suspicion. Maybe she brought that spy cam she wore as a necklace during that under-cover operation we had in Buffalo with a buyer. Or maybe she posed as one of these young women mingling with the Rich Boys, waiting to get trapped. But that would have been reckless. Dangerous.

Cinder was in a dark place, but *that?*

Once I reach the stairs, I set down my tray on an ornately carved wooden table, as if that's normal, and I calmly stride up the stairs. I'm looking for an office. Probably not behind one of the doors along the balconies. My guess is those are in use—a theory confirmed by a couple slipping out, faces flushed, clothes rumpled. They're smiling and striding back to the party, taking the stairs on the far side from me. *Strange.* This is looking more like a frat party than a brothel. Unless there's a weekend package Lord has for his guests.

I head up to the third level, hoping for some-thing that looks more office-like. A couple more doors line the short railing, but past that is a hallway that leads to some kind of gaming room—pool table, some old-fashioned arcade games, a table set with crystal chess pieces, and a big screen with a bank of recliners lined up like at the movies. I dead-end with that, and I'm about to back-track when I see a door next to a bar tucked in the corner. Sure enough, that opens into an office. The light automatically comes on. It's more of a den—floor-to-ceiling bookshelves, windows out into the breezy summer night, and an ostentatious desk opposite a couple chairs and a big leather couch.

Bingo.

I search the desk drawers—a couple are locked, but I pull out my pick kit, and it's easy to spring those free. *Nothing.* Just some antique personal items and a journal—no names, numbers, or incriminating dates, though. Not even in code. I leave that and turn to the computer on the built-in desk along the wall. It's password-protected, of course, but it's not like I came unprepared. I dig out a small flash drive loaded with software to override the operating system—a college girlfriend who's now a major security expert hooked me up, once I promised her I was white hatting, not breaking into the Pentagon. I slip it into the USB port and hard boot the computer. My friend's software overrides the reboot, kicking it into another operating system. I type in the command script I memorized, and it starts searching for files and images—anything that might be incriminating for a sex trafficker. I'm just scraping everything; I'll look through the files later from the comfort and safety of my apartment back in NYC.

While I'm waiting for the download, I check for secret drawers or hidden vaults in the bookcase. A waist-height panel that looks blank actually springs open with my nudge then slides out a lit-up tray. Nestled in white satin is an ancient leather book with a dragon etched in black metallic ink. It sparkles in the warm light of the den, and it's cool to the touch of my fingertip along the curving tail. Curiosity gets the better of me. I pick it up and unwrap the rough leather cord used to hold it shut. Inside are symbols I don't recognize—some of it looks Greek, and the rest has to be a language, but it's like none I've ever seen. I flip through the pages. The illustrations are more dragons, mostly black, but some silver and gold. There's a battle, one page to the next, fire and swords and flaming blue blasts of energy—

"Who the hell are you?"

I jump inside my skin and spin around. *Fuck.* I could have sworn I closed the door. But no. And

Nikolais Lord is standing in the doorway with a young woman who looks as shocked as he is, but only half as outraged. I clutch the book to my chest like that will somehow save me. "I… I was just curious…" *Fuck, fuck, fuck.* I helplessly gesture with the book. Is he armed? If he's armed, I'm *so* fucked—

"Go get Aleks," he says in a rough voice to the woman, never taking his eyes off me. She scurries out.

Dammit, I fucked this up. "I'm so sorry!" I say, going for the innocent catering server caught pilfering the client's stash of… what? Dragon lit? "I just love books, and you have so many, and I'll just put this one back, I'm sure it's special in this nice little drawer—" I turn my back to put the book away, sneaking a glance at the flash drive. *Copy Complete,* it says. Fucking hell, I need to grab that—

"I'll take that." The book is lifted out of my hands.

What? Lord is right next to me. I had my back turned for less than a second, and somehow, without a sound and way too freaking fast, he crossed the room. I lean away, heart skittering with the shock. "I was just going to put it—"

"You have no idea how precious this is." His eyes are lit with a dark fire. His gaze bores into mine, capturing me with its heat. The pictures online don't do him justice—the man is *intensely* beautiful. In a sexy, swarthy Greek kind of way. A dark scruff shadows his face, taking the edge off his beauty just enough to make him slightly rugged. And so, so sexy. Masculinity rolls off him like a wave that laps its tongue over my entire body. I take another step back, even more unsettled. Hotness is *not* a thing that rattles me.

He glares and turns to reverently place the book back in its cradle of white satin. As he's carefully sliding the drawer back in place, I edge backward, watching him, determined to yank the flash drive free. I flick my gaze to the computer and silently snag it—

His hand locks around my wrist and hauls me away from the computer with breathtaking strength. *But I got the drive.* I shove up into his chest, using his strength against him, then grab his collar and lift *up*. Surprise lights up his face, then I drop to the floor, collapsing under him, twisting and pulling him over my huddled form for the throw. He's *insanely* heavy—for a split second, I don't think he'll budge—but then he tumbles forward, over my hunched body, his own momentum taking him down. Then suddenly, I'm yanked with him. *He never let go.* Before I can blink, he's got me pinned, that massive weight holding me, a knee across my pelvis, my arms flat on the floor, useless. *Fuck.* It takes me a half-second to realize he *let* me throw him... just to get me here. Pinned. *Trapped.*

My breath is heaving, but panic is just starting to light up my heart.

"What the hell *are* you?" He says it with an open-mouthed grin like this is fucking funny, then he frowns at my hands pinned by my head. "What's that?" One still has the flash drive.

I'm trying to calm my breathing, trying to fight through the panic in my mind. What's the right answer to give? How do I get out of this? "Flash drive," I pant, stalling.

He eases up a little on the pressure. He's not winded. At all. His frown grows deeper. "No... *this.*" He hauls my hand off the floor—the one *without* the flash drive—and his grip is like being locked to a *wall.* He holds my wrist up for me to see. He's dead serious now, but I have no idea what he means.

"It's... my hand."

"Is it a tattoo?" he demands.

What the fuck? I don't have any... Oh. "Birthmark." He's talking about the ragged half-circle birthmark I've had on the inside of my wrist ever since I was born.

The wide-eyed look on his face sends a chill down my back. Why the hell does that matter? What is this guy's problem? I imagine strange tattoo fetishes. The horrible fact that I've fucked all this up *so* badly is sinking a chill deep into my stomach.

He drags his gaze from the marvel of my birthmark and gives me a crazed look. "I can't decide whether to kiss you or lock you up."

Fuck. "Kiss me, and there will be blood. Not mine, either."

The crazy on his face is blasted away by a smile. A bright shining smile that, *fuck me,* is beautiful on this insane, gorgeous man. He's got me pinned to the floor, grinning like a lunatic, his hair mussed from the throw, with a shine of excitement in his eyes… and I'm thinking about how hot he is? Did I take a knock to the head? But suddenly, I'm not afraid of him. Like I should be. I *really* should be. He's probably going to lock me up *and* kiss me. Or worse. Much worse. But he's got this goofy, disarming look on his face now like he's a little kid who just unlocked a hidden treasure box and discovered a pile of gold.

He eases off me and brings me with him, his

iron grip on my wrist as he stands—as if I'm some rag doll he can haul around without thinking. I've never met someone with that kind of muscle—just raw, pure strength. The kind you get from lifting… something. Not weights. More like boulders. I don't know where he carries it, either. His body seems muscular, but not body-builder territory. Besides, those guys are weak compared to the very surprising and totally unexpected, in many ways, Nikolais Lord.

"I thought you might say that," he says, and I've almost forgotten what I said.

Oh, right—I threatened to bloody him. Smart.

He's still got a lock on my wrist. "What's your name?" He's asking like we've just met at a coffee bar.

"Excuse me?" I'm uncertain where this is going.

He tilts his head and gives me a chastising look. "I'll find out. This will just make it easier."

On *him?* Or on me? Unclear. But we're negotiating. Maybe. "Ember Dubois." I hesitate, but since he'll just look me up… "Reporter for World News. I've won a few awards. Pretty big deal, actually. People will notice if I disappear. They'll come looking."

The goofiness on his face slowly evaporates with my words. A dark scowl settles in.

Someone comes to the door behind me. The woman is back, and she's brought a man with her—it's the hot rich guy from downstairs who noticed my nametag. "What's going on, Niko?"

"Take her to the dungeon."

The fuck? I whip a look back to him.

He holds out his hand for the flash drive. I press my lips together and drop it in his palm. His friend suddenly looms behind me. He gives Lord a pinched look like he's not quite sure of this plan, but when Lord finally releases my wrist, his goon just gestures me toward the door. I follow his unspoken command.

What the hell was I thinking, doing this on my own? I don't have backup. *No one* will come looking for me. Well, my editor might miss me... a couple weeks from now. By then, I'll be decomposing. Or trafficked. Which means I'll be dead because I know me—I'll fight my way out of that as long as I'm drawing breath.

I fucked this up *so* bad.

TWO

Niko

"Are you sure it's the mark?" Aleksandr asks.

"No, I'm not sure." I scowl at him. "How could I be sure? Have you ever seen a mark in real life?"

"No." Because of course, he hasn't. It's insanely rare.

I run both hands through my hair and glare at the door to the dungeon. It's in the basement—a very well-lit and modern basement—and one of the few places in the lair where we actually can lock people up. The doors of the castle only lock from the *inside*—for privacy. Ms. Ember Dubois is in the kind of "restraint" you get out of with a safe word, but I'm not sure what's really "safe" with a woman like her. It's possible I've already screwed this up by handcuffing her to the wall—the panic in her beautiful amber-green eyes clawed at me the whole march down here and especially when she saw the room—but the less explanation, the better. At least until Aleks and I get a handle on this. And without her way-too-intelligent mind reading between the lines.

Because I'm lost in this. Failing once again as the leader I'm supposed to be.

Aleks is flipping through the pages of the Μύθος του Δράκου. The *Mýthos tou Drákou* is the only thing I rescued from the fire that consumed our home lair outside Athens two hundred years ago. Dragons are impervious to fire, but the fire that consumed our family and friends was no ordinary flame. By the time we returned, almost everyone was dead. We had little time to save anything and could only take what we could carry —my friends desolately searched for personal items, but I went straight for the book. The original text is ancient, far older than any dragon living even then, but this translation had modern Greek mixed with the original. Which was good because we were just kids then, barely twenty. None of us knew a damn thing, and we'd all slacked off when learning the lore. I was the only one who'd taken my Dragon Tongue studies seriously. The book is all we've had—all *I've* had—to guide an entire people. What's left of one, anyway.

"I can't find the part about the mark." The frustration is making Aleks, my cousin who is really more of a brother to me, tear at the pages with uncharacteristic impatience.

It makes me flinch, so I just recite it. "The Dragon Spirited bear no outward sign, no mark or visage or color. You shall know them by their hearts when they open. Once in a hundred years, a Dragon Spirit of special destiny will bear the mark of the broken soul that lies within."

Aleks stops and stares. "You memorized it?"

"Of course, I fucking memorized it." I relieve him of the book and quickly turn to the page with the illustration. I give it back, but it's clear to see— the same jagged half-circle, the mark of the broken soul, that Ember Dubois was apparently born with. "She has to be a Dragon Spirit."

He's still staring at the ancient illustration as if that will make it change into something else. He looks up. "Maybe it's just a coincidence."

"Really?" I sigh and rub my hand across my face, wiping away the urge to snarl. "You didn't see her take me down. Or try to." I could *feel* the dragon spirit inside her. But I don't say this. It's just a gut reaction, nothing real.

Aleks's eyebrows hike up. "Did you kiss her?"

I glare at him. "She was *fighting* me."

Then he dashes a look to the door. "Maybe I could—"

A growl surges up from deep in my chest. "Don't even think about it."

He looks at me like I'm insane. "You don't know who she's meant for. Or if she's even Dragon Spirited at all."

"She is." It comes out harsh. I suck in a breath. "Aleks. My brother. We've got a situation here, and I need you to keep it in your pants long enough to help me."

His expression scrunches up like he's offended. No... *hurt.* "I'm trying, Niko."

It stabs me through the heart. Because Aleks has had my back for two hundred years, through countless women, countless false hopes, and now one beautiful fiery spirit tangles with me in the den, and I'm biting his head off? He deserves better than that.

I shake my head and drop my gaze. "Sorry."

"You *like* this one." He's back to the gentle spirit I've known all my life.

I give him a guilty sideways glance. I *shouldn't*— that's the unspoken rule of the lair. Every dragon gets a chance at a possible mate before me. Not because it matters—there's only one match, one broken soul in all the universe that's a dragon's perfect other half—but it would be embarrassing to have your mate be the reject of the Lord of the Lair. It's an old tradition, meant to soothe the egos of vain male dragons and keep the peace, but we've clung to the old traditions. Or rather I have— because it was all we had when everything else was taken from us.

Aleks lifts an eyebrow. "You're fond of a woman who's possibly *stealing* from us."

"Now you're back on point." I rub my temple and shove away the guilt and the protocol. We're in new territory here. "She's a reporter for World News. And a *good* one." It took all of ten seconds to verify her story. Pulitzer-prize-winning investigative journalist. Known for hard-hitting pieces out of war-torn countries. "She'll expose us. And you know we can't afford that." We're barely hanging on as it is. More of us are dying every day.

"But if she's a Dragon Spirit…" The hope is back in his eyes. And I can't help but share it. "We haven't had a new mating in twenty years. The men are losing hope. Even the young ones."

"I know." I rub my face with both hands again. "But if we bring her in—if we tell her everything— that could be the end of us."

"You haven't failed us yet, Niko." He claps his hand on my shoulder. I know he means it. I know he *believes* it. But the truth is I've been failing them all from the beginning.

I pull in a breath and keep that to myself. No sense in shattering Aleks's faith, even if it's misplaced. "So… we're agreed. We've got to tell her."

"It's got to be you." His expression falls serious. "Fuck protocol. There's no dragon in this lair I trust to romance a human more than you. And there's too much riding on this."

His words surge emotion through my chest. Excitement. *Possessiveness.* Because I already knew I couldn't let any other dragon get close to her. That was clear the moment I had her underneath me in my den, sassy and outraged. But to hear the approval in Aleks's voice relieves the guilt nipping at that sudden *need* to make her mine. She's beautiful, strong, smart as hell—is that it? Because there's no way to know if she's my other half, not yet. Not without the kiss. Am I just being an asshole dragon who wants to hoard the most alluring treasure that's walked through our doors in a decade? Probably.

I shove aside the doubts—no time for those. "Let's do this." I push open the door to the dungeon and stride in... only to nearly stumble over my own damn feet. Ember has somehow climbed to the top of the St. Andrew's Cross that I've hand-cuffed her to—I only cuffed one hand, my obvious mistake—and she's trying to break the cross by bracing her feet to the wall and prying the wooden cross free.

"Holy shit," Aleks whispers, but it catches her attention.

She grimaces then gives one last, desperate shove with her bare feet—her flat shoes are lying on the floor—but the cross remains stubbornly attached. Then she swings down, and I see the pain flash across her face as her wrist contorts in the cuff. It's leather, and the red marks on her skin show how much she's abusing her body, trying to get free.

Fuck. I practically fly across the room, nearly shifting out wings, my need to reach her is so urgent. I vault over the edging bench and its various restraints and pin her cuffed hand to the wall. "What the *hell* are you doing?" I grab the chain that binds the cuff to the cross and rip it straight out of the wood.

Her eyes go wide as I step back. She cradles her injured wrist to her chest.

I want to go to her, comfort her, but I just grind out, "Aleks, the key."

He hustles forward in a flash. She flinches away from him, so he just hands it over. She tries, but the damn lock is built to require two hands. Part of the kink, I guess. I'm not into the dungeon, and it's strictly for play, but I've heard the devices can be a challenge. She makes a small sound of frustration, and I'm drawn forward like it's a physical compulsion. She eyes me warily.

"Let me help." I keep my voice soft. What was I thinking, leaving her like this? Without explanation? I'm worse than an asshole. That's bordering on monstrous. All because I was indecisive. Another failure of leadership to add to the pile.

She tries the key again, then grimaces and offers up her wrist and the cuff. I make quick work and fling the offending hardware away. Her skin is red and raw.

"I didn't mean for…" I wince. "Are you okay?"

"Fuck you and your little boy fantasies." She's *pissed*—and has every right to be—but I can hear the tremor of fear in those words she's throwing at me.

Shame heats my face. "This is not my fantasy." I flick a look at the broken wood, then back to her. "And I assure you I'm not a *little boy* in any sense." Although I'm clearly a fool. "Please accept my apology for detaining you in this way. It was… thoughtless." I grind my teeth with how accurate that is.

Her expression is wary again. "So, I'm free to go then." She flicks a look at Aleks, who's retreated halfway to the door.

"The question is, why were you here in the first place?"

She rubs her wrist and glares at me. Because I'm obviously not releasing her yet. The birthmark on her other wrist draws my attention. "I don't know what you expected to find on my computer, but whatever it was…" I drag my gaze up to meet hers. "I'll tell you what you want to know. But then I need your help."

Her beautiful eyes light up, curiosity dousing the anger. "Help for what?"

"You first." Somehow, I have to fix this mess. And I can start by giving her whatever she was seeking. Because it wasn't to indulge in the weekly parties we throw, trying to bring in as many potential mates as we can.

Uncertainty clouds her face again.

"You're a reporter." I gesture for her to come sit with me on the edging bench. She's having none of that, so I stay standing. "You were after something. A story. To be honest, looking at your credentials, I wouldn't have figured you for covering high society social events. And I don't know what dirt you expected to find on my hard drive."

She narrows her eyes. "I was looking for my sister."

My eyebrows lift. "On my computer?"

"She's disappeared. Her planner said she was coming here."

What? Could she have come through? Gotten recruited and passed on to one of the other lairs? I frown and twist to Aleks. He shrugs. I swing back to Ember. "Do you have a picture? We could check if anyone's seen her."

Her expression pinches in. "You're serious."

"If your sister is missing, I'd be more than happy to help you find her."

The pinched look is still there. "Unless you trafficked her out already."

My mouth drops open, and I'm momentarily

speechless. I snap it closed. "So that's what you think," I say tightly. But everything clicks into place. I know the rumors—it's impossible to avoid them, as much as we try to keep a low profile. Some women, once they enter our world, don't want to go back. And then there are the women we rescue. That's a lot of unexplained traffic through the castle —but not the human trafficking that Ember Dubois is apparently investigating.

"Is that a denial?" Ember lifts her chin, but her voice is cool. She thinks the worst of us—of *me*.

I step back. Maybe this is a mistake. Maybe my fervent desire for salvation for my people is making me see solutions where there are only problems. I glance at Aleks, and he's looking uncertain. "I've never held a woman against her will in my life," I say to her. "Except you, briefly. And that was a mistake. Notwithstanding the fact that you were breaking into my office." I swing my arm wide to the door. "You're free to go."

Her expression opens, and she blinks. Looks at the door. Hesitates. "You really haven't seen my sister?"

I grimace. "Like I said, if you have a picture, I can—"

"She looks like me."

"Something maybe a *little* more specific—"

"Exactly like me." She plants her hands on her hips, suddenly not going anywhere. "We're twins."

Everything in me stills. "What did you say?"

"Identical twins. If you haven't seen *me* before, then…" She stops at the look on my face.

I turn, wide-eyed, to Aleks. *"Two* of them."

He's shaking his head, fast. "Just because one is, doesn't mean the other…" He frowns at her. "Your sister—does she have the birthmark?"

Ember's face scrunches up with a *What the fuck?* look. "Okay, *yes…* for what it's worth…"

Holy shit. Aleks is struggling for words, but I know just what to say. I turn back to Ember. "We *will* find your sister." It's a bit too intense, judging by the freaked look on her face.

"On second thought…" She slowly backs toward the door. "Maybe I'll just go."

"Ember, wait!" I lurch toward her, then stop as she tenses. This is getting away from me. "Please, just… if I tell you what's *really* happening here, will you stay? Let us help you find your sister? All I ask is that you keep it out of the news. You'll understand why once I explain."

Her pinched look is fierce. But she's not moving

toward the door anymore. "I can't make any promises."

I look to Aleks, but this is all on me. The risk. The lives of everyone in the lair. I face Ember and say, "We're dragons. All of us."

"The fuck are you talking about?" She thinks I'm crazy. Of course.

So I transform in front of her.

THREE

Ember

I STUMBLE BACK, FALL ON MY ASS, AND... JUST STAY down.

Because a fucking *dragon* looms over me.

He's big—he has to bend to fit in the room—and his body is like a small tank. The sound of his long tail swishing slowly along the carpet, nearly hidden from view, sends a full-body shudder through me. His black scales glisten, and the claws on his hands and feet, now elongated and deadly-looking, are at least six inches and curved at the tip. My brain is completely on auto-pilot, just *staring* at him. His serpentine neck lowers his bony-ridged head to my feet, eyes closed, like he's... *bowing* to me. Only then do I see the wings—tucked against his back, folded like a bat's and covered with the same ebony scales, but then… feathers at the tips? They blend with the scales, all black as midnight, and rustle slightly. I can't figure out why they're moving until I hear the slow and steady breath in and out of the dragon's giant lungs.

A fucking *dragon*. Right in front of me.

Just when I think I should be screaming or running, he turns human. So fast that, had I blinked, I would have missed it. He's standing on two legs again, only now he's naked—and sporting a massive erection. He didn't lie about the *not little* part. His clothes are in a pile on the floor. Somehow, I missed those when he was a *dragon* taking up half the room. But now that he's a man again, I can't take my eyes off him, either. The beautiful face is just the icing on top of a stunning Olympic-level-hot beefcake. Under all those fancy clothes, he's made of pure muscle. And *endowed*… holy shit, it's making my mouth water, which is *not* an appropriate reaction to the situation. It's the same as back in his office when the intense *maleness* of him lapped heat all over my body.

"Sorry for the show." His voice is rough. He grabs his clothes and turns his back to slide on his pants, which gives me a spectacular view of his finely-sculpted ass. Every part of this man is beauti-

ful. I'm still swallowing the dryness in my mouth—
still completely out of words—when he turns back
to face me. He starts to slide on his white shirt then
sees the sleeve is shattered. Just shreds hang from it.
He fucking *growls* then throws the thing to the floor
in disgust. "Apparently, I'm out of practice." He just
stands there with his fabulously sculpted chest and
bare feet, and I have to consciously close my mouth.

"Turning dragon takes… *practice?*" I croak out. I
can't believe I'm saying those words, but I'm not
into denying what I see with my own eyes.

Nikolais Lord is a *real-life* dragon.

I struggle up to standing—I think better on my
feet, not sprawled on the floor.

"Yes." His face is strangely blank. Like he's
holding back a thousand emotions. "I imagine you
have questions."

"I have *so many* questions." My heart skips a
beat. I should be afraid. I should be screaming my
fucking head off and running—because the talons
on this guy, not to mention his fucking fangs—but
all I've got raging through my head is an insane
need *to know.* What is this? How is this possible?
How does it all work? Why, for the love of cable
news, is he showing this to *me?* I've never been able
to hold back the curiosity beast when it rears up, no

matter the danger. That was what made me so good in the field, on location, embedded with troops—wherever the story was.

The story is definitely *here.*

But the glower on Lord's face is just getting darker. "You can't tell anyone, Ember."

Shit. He did say something about that. "Sure. Of course." I'd say anything at this point to get *more* on this.

"And we need to talk." Now he just looks weary. "But not here."

A small bubble of alarm trickles up from somewhere sane in my brain. "Where are we going?"

But he speaks to the other guy instead. "I need a shirt."

"You can have mine." He starts to quickly unbutton, then just hauls the black silk shirt over his head and tosses it to Lord, who slides it on.

I can't help staring at his friend—Aleks is his name—because he's *built,* just like Lord. "Wait, did you say... you're *all* dragons?"

"Try to keep that to yourself while we're walking through the castle." Lord seems testy like he's still bothered by having to put on the new shirt. He finishes that then kneels down to quickly slide on his shoes.

I look away since my scrutiny seems to bother him. Instead, I give Aleks an appreciative look. "Are you a black dragon, too?" I say it like it's the hottest thing I can think of. Which, to be honest, isn't far wrong. My mind is *on fire* with this.

Panic flits across Aleks's face like I'm not supposed to talk to him, just Lord. "Um… yeah? I mean, most of the lair—" He cuts himself off and dashes a look to Lord.

I lift an eyebrow. "Lair?" I pivot to Lord again. "Is that what you call your castle?"

He's done with his shoes. "This isn't going to be easy for you, is it?" There's a little menace behind it, and I try to reel in my rabid reporter. There's something dark in all this—we're talking hidden dragons, sex parties, lots and lots of money—and it would be smart to be at least *a little* careful before plunging in headfirst. If that's even possible for me.

"Just dying inside of curiosity," I say, trying to lighten things. Plus, it's true.

It works. A tiny smile flashes across his face then disappears. "Come with me."

My wrist is still smarting from the leather hand-cuff, but all that is forgiven if this is what he was protecting. *A world of secret dragon people.* How can he keep such a thing secret? Especially with all the people circulating through the castle? And what's up with that? The questions keep tumbling through my head, but I keep it zipped while we stride down the basement hallway to an elevator at the end. Aleks trails behind us, but he doesn't come inside.

"See if anyone's seen her sister," Lord says, voice rough again.

Aleks whips out his phone and takes a quick picture of me as the elevator door is closing.

"You really meant it," I say, impressed now in the context of what little I know. "I mean, when you said you wanted to help find her."

He's staring at the elevator doors. "I doubt she's been to the castle." He swings a look to me as the elevator slows. "Someone like you wouldn't have gone unnoticed."

I'm not sure what he means. "She's not like me." I frown as the door opens, and he waits for me to go first. "I mean, she looks like me, but you can tell the difference."

"Meaning she doesn't break and enter?"

I scowl. "There was no *breaking* involved."

He smirks and directs me down a hallway as elaborately decorated as the rest of the castle. There are several side doors and one large golden door at the end. A dragon is carved in the panel, and its tail wraps around the top of the door. He slips a keycard out of his pants pocket and waves it at the door—it clicks and swings open on its own.

Okay, then. The reclusive dragon billionaire is bringing me to his private quarters? Just to talk, like he said, I'm sure. Although I don't mind seeing his naked and very pleasing form pop up in my head. Is that where this is going? I can't say that I'd mind, although what exactly is the procedure for sleeping with a half-man, half-beast? That stirs way too much excitement between my legs—and I need to focus on the sexiness of this *story,* not the lickable body of the guy attached to it.

Lord walks me through his apartment, which is beyond lavish in décor—white rugs, gilt mirrors, marble, and black-and-white leather everywhere. Very modern and pristine and expensive as hell. Where *does* Lord get his money? All my research showed was inherited money from his American-born father and old-money from Greece. Lord opens a large, glass double-door and ushers me out onto a wide balcony. It overlooks the water, which is sparkling dark; the moon has yet to rise, and the islands are far enough apart that any light from the nearest is too dim to shine on the water. But a million stars fill the sky—you can't see anything like this in the city.

He's watching me soak it in. "Would you like to take a ride?"

I frown. "A ride—"

He shifts again, and my heart lurches with surprise. He's as dark as the night and so close I can touch him. Which I would except my whole body seems locked up from the shock. He rumbles a little —like a storm somewhere in the depths of his volu- minous chest. Then he dips his head again, only this time he settles all the way down, limbs folded until he's flat against the balcony.

"This is *the ride?*" My voice is a whisper. Is he fucking serious?

He twists his head back on that long, serpentine neck. I shy away from that snout full of dagger-like teeth, but he's just shuffling me with his nose toward his back. Am I supposed to climb up? How am I supposed to hold on? What if I fall?

Cause of death: falling from a midnight-black dragon.

Not that anyone would ever know.

But who am I kidding? I'm not passing this up.

I'm a little tentative at first—how does one mount a dragon?—but then the scales aren't as slippery as they look, and they're warm, and I finally manage to scramble up his folded front leg and straddle his neck with his wings behind me. He rises slowly, just straightening his legs, then suddenly, his wings unfold and *flap*... and we're in the air! My knees clench tight onto his neck, and I desperately grab at a bony ridge that's just right for gripping. I hold tight, both hands and legs, and an answering rumble shudders deep inside his body. The sound is carried away by the wind in my face. *I am flying... on a dragon.* The stars above and the water and inky blackness of islands below make it feel like we're alone in the universe—just the wind, the hum of the dragon between my legs, and a distant whip-poor-will cry in the night.

I almost forget to breathe... and when I do, it's gasping and erratic. I don't want it to end, but it quickly does. We drop fast, my stomach left behind as we swoop and alight on another balcony, this one dark and made of crumbling stone. The dragon—Nikolais Lord, I remind myself, because this is all just too crazy—kneels down again, flattening out so I can dismount. Which I quickly do, breathless and feeling *alive* in a way that makes my heart stutter even when I'm standing still. I notice he's carried his clothes in his talons just before he shifts again.

This time, I turn away and face the water, which is peeking through the night canopy of trees, giving him privacy to get dressed, but not before I see that he's once again at attention. Does shifting always give him a hard-on? Or is it something about *me?* Which is ridiculous, but the questions about all this are bursting in my head. And the ache between my legs is reminding me how long it's been since I properly had a man between them. If Nikolais Lord can thrill my private parts with a dragon ride, what could that world-class body do as a human in bed?

Goosebumps rise over my entire body.

Holy shit, Ember, pull it together. I wipe the naked lust off my face—I hope—and turn back to face Lord.

He's smiling as he buttons his shirt. "You took that in stride."

"You didn't rip your shirt this time."

He scowls, but it doesn't dim his smile. "Come inside." He tips his head, leaving his shoes on the balcony and throwing open the door that led to it. With a snap of his fingers, the place lights up inside. There's a canopy draped bed, which sends a flush through me, but Lord heads toward a red velvet couch. The furnishings all seem ancient but well-kept. The place is clean and maintained, unlike the crumbling stone of the balcony.

"This is a little retreat of mine." He casually takes a seat on the couch and pats the cushion for me to sit. As I slowly sink into the crushed velvet, he continues, "It was the first home we built in America. I spent a lot of nights here, *alone,*" he emphasizes, "trying to figure out what to do next."

"I thought you were born in America." I take a closer look at the furnishings. They're antiques from a different era.

Lord is frowning like he expects better from me.

My eyebrows slowly lift to the top of my head. "All of it is a cover story."

His smile is slow but broad. "Which part do you want to know first?"

My heart rate kicks up a notch. I slip off my shoes—now barefoot like him—and fold my legs up on the couch, fidgeting into place while I sort through what I want to know. What I'm dying to know. "How old are you?"

"Two hundred and nineteen." His eyes sparkle. The lights in the room are modern, fake candles on the wall.

"Shut up. You look thirty."

"We don't age much after that."

How does he expect me to believe that? Then again... why not? "This is your first home in America—where was your home before that?"

Some of the sparkle fades. "I was born in a lair outside Athens."

"Athens, *Greece*," I verify. When he nods, I add, "Why come here?"

He frowns and draws in a breath, letting it out slow. "Doesn't take you long to get to the heart of the matter, does it, Ms. Dubois?"

"Call me Ember."

That brings a smile to his face—a damn sexy smile. "I'm Niko to my friends."

My heart does a small jitter. "Am I your friend?" We are definitely *something* here.

"I'd like you to be." His gaze drops for just a second to my lips then bounces back to my eyes. "It's safer that way. For *me*." He's searching my eyes now, asking for something without asking.

I'm transfixed. "What does a rich man who's also a dangerously powerful dragon have to fear?"

He dips his head and reaches for my hand. I let him because, honestly, every inch of my skin is lit up just being near enough to touch. He takes my scraped-up wrist in one hand and rubs his thumb lightly over the marks. "I didn't mean for this to happen," he says softly, then peers at me. "Will you let me fix it?"

"Fix it?" *Damn,* who's doing the seducing here? I'm supposed to be wheedling information out of him. But whatever works… "Fix it how?"

His sexy smile and lit-up eyes capture me while he scoots even closer on the couch. He pulls my hand up to his face, my wrist by his lips like he's going to kiss it, but he doesn't. "Dragon saliva has some mild healing properties. All of our bodily fluids do. That's part of the longevity of our kind." He holds my gaze while he brushes his lips across the inside of my wrist. Then his tongue slips out, and the tip traces figure-eights across my skin.

"Are you kidding me?" I breathe. It's so hot, I'm in danger of melting. Worse, I might throw myself on him right here on the couch.

He grins and laps one more time at my wrist, then lets me go.

I nearly topple forward on the couch, pulling my dignity and my wrist back only at the last second. It's tingly and wet and cool with the slight breeze off the balcony but when I look at it… the red marks are gone. Pretty sure my eyes are bugging out.

"There's a lot to know about us."

When I look up, the smirk and the smolder are gone. "I want to know it all."

He frowns. "I'm still not sure I can trust you, Ms. Dubois. *Ember.*"

I scowl because he has me completely off balance. And I'm not sure he's wrong. How can I possibly keep any of this a secret? "What happens to me if I don't keep quiet? Just so we're clear about that." I'm thinking roasted journalist on a stick. Do dragons eat humans? Or just the traitorous ones?

He nods. "That's the right question to ask." He leans back, breaking up our cozy space, and takes another deep breath. Then he meets my searching gaze again. "We have enemies. They're nearly immortal, much longer-lived than we are, yet they hate us. Two hundred years ago, they waged a genocidal war against dragon kind. Not really a *war,* actually. They wiped us out in a day. Simultaneous strikes on all dozen lairs across the planet. It took us a while to figure that out—communication was much less efficient back then."

My mouth is hanging open again. "But... why? And *who?*" Immortal beings? A whisper in the back of my brain warns me that I'm not keeping *any* journalistic skepticism here. But I can't help it. This is all too fantastical to know what not to believe.

"They're the Vardigah, a kind of dark elves. They have a natural enemy—the Dhogerthu, the light elves—and they kept the Vardigah in check forever, at least as far back as dragon lore goes. As a result, the Vardigah mostly left us alone. But something must have happened to the Dhogerthu—maybe the Vardigah finally defeated them? They both live in a separate realm. Not easy to reach. And needless to say, we don't go there voluntarily. As for why... well, that part we know fairly well." He leans forward again, peering into my eyes. "But this part is most sensitive of all, Ember. I need to know you understand the stakes here. If you announce to the world you've found hidden dragons in the Thousand Islands in upstate New York, the Vardigah will find us. And they'll destroy every last one of us."

I'm shaking my head, not because I don't believe him—I do. It's not as if the world isn't filled with genocidal monsters who mostly lack the ability to enact their evil desires. And some *do* have the means. There's a lot of killing in the world. I've seen it up close. Why would magical creatures be any different?

"I wouldn't put anyone at risk for a story. Certainly not an entire people." That I can promise easily enough. I need to make sure this is *actually* true—my journalistic sense is rearing its practical brain again—but if it is, I'll take the secret of these dragon people to the grave.

He smiles, and it's sweet, almost goofy. The same smile he had in the office when he had me pinned to the floor. "I knew you were Dragon Spirited."

"Huh?"

He leans back, but the smile doesn't go away. Then he rubs his hand across his mouth, almost like he's trying to wipe away the giddiness. "My people have prided themselves on being noble of spirit. To be *dragon* is to fight for justice in the world. For what's good and right."

I cock my head to the side. "Kinda full of your-selves, are you?"

He laughs, but it's light-hearted. "We can be." Then he leans forward and whispers, "We like to hoard things, too. The more precious, the better."

"Okay, that's just funny." But I'm not entirely sure he's joking.

"We have other powers, but most of them come once we're mated." The humor is gone now, and he's watching my reaction.

"I'm sorry… *mated?*" My curiosity springs to attention. "How does that work?"

"It'll sound strange to you," he warns, but I recognize a tease when I hear one. "It's not like human mating rituals."

"Then you absolutely need to tell me." I'm fighting my own smirk. And the rush that's heating my body. Whatever kink the dragons are into—they had a hell of a dungeon down there, so I will guess that's part of it—I could easily be all-in for exploring it with the hot Mr. Nikolais Lord. If this can't be a story, then all bets are off; besides, there are plenty of secret sources I've romped with before because why not? There are only so many chances you'll have to bang an agent of the CIA.

"I'll tell you…" His eyes are drinking me in now. "But I doubt you'll believe it."

"Try me." He's killing me with this lead-up.

He surprises me again by reaching for my hand, but this time, it's the other one—the one with the birthmark. *Uh oh.* Here it comes.

"When a new dragon is formed, his soul is broken in two." He traces the circle on my wrist with his fingertip. "The other half is born in a human woman. We call her Dragon Spirited, and she's the one who is destined to become his mate.

Only when they've been joined again, can he reach his full powers. And the woman as well—only when her spirit is whole will her dragon powers manifest in her body."

My heart is doing that jittery thing. "You're saying she becomes a dragon."

"Yes." That goofy look takes over his face. "Very few of the Dragon Spirited are marked—it's exceedingly rare, in fact—but *you* are, Ember. This…" He lightly taps my birthmark. "Reveals your true nature."

I pull back my hand. "Yeah… I don't think so." This is suddenly feeling like an elaborate setup.

He leans back and props his arm on the back of the couch. "I knew you wouldn't believe it."

I scowl at him. "It's a little strange."

He shrugs. And he did say that, too. "As for why that matters… only a mated dragon comes into his full powers. One of which is a venom capable of killing even a Vardigah."

"That's why they tried to wipe you out?" That part makes sense. Maybe.

"Not only us—the witches too."

"There are witches *too?*" For the love of news hour…

He grins. "Think about it, Ms. Dubois. If the

other half of your soul lived in one very specific person on the planet… and if that person was the one and only person you could ever hope to mate with… how would you find them?"

I frown. "That's a logistical nightmare."

"Indeed." He almost laughs but reins it in. "Which is why we need the witches. Their divination powers can identify the Dragon Spirited among the humans—they would, in essence, tell us who our soul mates were. In trade, we kept them supplied with many magical artifacts, including on occasion, some of those bodily fluids." His humor fades. "It was a good life. A life I thought would be mine. I'd assumed…" He peers off through the open doors to the balcony. "One should never assume."

My chest tightens. "Wait, so… the witches are gone, and most of the dragons, too, and you don't know who your soul mates are, so you can't mate, which I'm guessing means you can't make baby dragons…" The horror of it finally sinks in.

He turns back with a pained smile. "Yes, we are dying out, Ms. Dubois."

FOUR

Niko

EMBER'S BEEN QUIET EVER SINCE I TOLD HER THE stark truth.

My people won't last much longer.

That stopped the barrage of questions—in fact, she's been quieter than any other twenty-minute stretch in the short time I've known her. I asked if she had more questions, but she waved me off, stepping out onto the balcony to stare off into the night. Eventually, I offered her a ride back to the castle, which she accepted with a wordless nod. The heat of her riding on my neck, clenching me with her legs, makes my blood sing and my cock ache, but doing anything about that is a long way off—probably never. I might have blown this already, unsettling her with too much, too fast, and I haven't even explained what comes next. What I need from her.

She's silent the entire ride.

I land as gently as I can then sink to the floor to let her dismount. She drifts inside my apartment, her brow furrowed. I wait until she's out of sight to shift, then hastily dress—no need to flash her again. That part was probably unsettling enough *before* she knew dragons mated with women—specifically women like her. Not that she knows how special she is. Or believes any of it.

Her silence is killing me—have I screwed this up already?

"Can I get you something to drink?" I'm still buttoning the cuffs of Aleks's shirt. At least I've gotten my shifting under control again. It's been so long since I've had to shift out of clothes. Normally, I just disrobe for my weekly retreat from the castle and all the problems of the world. I rarely have to impress a human woman who doesn't know a thing about our kind. By the time the potential mates reach me, they've already been with most of the lair.

She's not answering me, just staring at the painting above the fireplace. It's a rendering of the lair in Athens. I painted it from memory.

"Ember?" I'm starting to think something is terribly wrong.

She touches the gilded frame with just her fingertips. "Is this your home?"

"Yes." She's sharp. And fearless. Not to mention gorgeous with that long dark-brown hair, porcelain skin, and a body that's lethal *and* sexy as hell. Whoever her mate is, he'll be one lucky dragon when she finds him.

She turns frowning. "Do you ever go back?"

"No."

She nods, not asking for an explanation.

I like it better when she's barraging me with questions. "My life is here now. With my brother dragons. There are three other lairs—one in Europe, two in Asia. None are the original ones that were destroyed. They're all much smaller, like ours. We're the largest at forty dragons strong. Most seek out the support of a lair, but some dragons have gone rogue, just circulating through the human world. We're all trying to rebuild."

"Trying to find your mates." Her eyes are wide, solemn.

"Yes." Which loosens the tension in my chest a little. She's giving me a chance to explain. Which means maybe I haven't messed this up completely.

"We bring as many women through as we can plausibly manage, then determine if they're the soul mate of someone in the lair. If not, they may circulate out to the other lairs."

She frowns and rubs the broken-circle birthmark, but I can see her curiosity spark back to life. "I don't understand. You said my birthmark was rare. If these women don't have it, then how can you tell if someone is Dragon Spirited? And if they are, how do you know which dragon is their soul mate?"

I step closer and gently take her hand, holding her wrist up between us. "It would be so much easier if every Dragon Spirit had a mark like yours." I release her. "There are two steps to a mating. In the first, the Dragon Spirit is revealed by a connection—an *intimate* connection. Each half of the soul recognizes the other, but only if they are laid bare."

Her eyes narrow. "*Sex.* You have sex with lots of women to find out if they're your soul mate."

I grin. "Well, that would work, too. But usually, a kiss is sufficient."

Her face scrunches up. "A kiss? Like in the fairy tales. You kiss Snow White, and she wakes up to be a dragon."

My laugh erupts like a hiccup. "Uh, no... not exactly?" I shake my head. "I've never heard it described that way." I try to tame my smile. "But no. I couldn't steal a kiss. Or force one for that matter. It has to be a True Kiss."

"I'm sorry, a what now?" She's scowling at me like I'm having fun with her, making this stuff up. Which I'm not, but I've seen worse reactions. Just like she flew on a dragon's back as if it were a stroll in the park, she's taking this all in tremendous stride. Which just convinces me more of her dragon nature.

I tilt my head and peer at her. "A True Kiss is one that opens your heart and makes it soar. Don't tell me you've never had a kiss like that."

Her expression opens again, becoming softer. "Once or twice."

I smile, but it's painful. "I've had hundreds. More, actually, but I stopped counting. Each time, I open my soul, hoping it will find its other half. Obviously, that hasn't happened yet."

"You're not mated?" She seems breathless.

I huff a laugh. "I would have thought that was obvious." I give her a pointed look.

Her eyebrows lift, and an *Ohhh* expression takes over. "You're supposed to give me a True Kiss."

"A True Kiss is *shared,* not given." I can't quite suppress the smile.

She scowls again. "Hang on. I thought you said my mark already shows I'm one of these Dragon Spirits. You don't need a kiss to see that."

"A True Kiss doesn't reveal whether you're Dragon Spirited; it would only reveal whether you're *my* soul mate." And I'm *so* tempted to just close the distance between us and kiss her now. So very tempted. But I know she's not ready. And pushing too fast is far worse than waiting too long. Too fast, and she might reject it all … and not just me. She's giving me a suspicious look like she expects me to jump over and plant one on her. "I highly doubt I'm lucky enough to be the one," I say, trying to bring down that expectation. "I'm not supposed to convince you to kiss me, Ember. I'm supposed to convince you to kiss every one of my brother dragons until you find the one who's your mate."

Her eyes go wide and then she blinks, once, twice, her body jolting a little each time as if the thought is delivering shocks to her mind. "Every… one… what the fuck, I'm not doing that!"

I try not to wince. "I know it's all so sudden and overwhelming. I just want you to consider…" I stop because my phone is buzzing in my pocket, and there's no way anyone would be interrupting me right now if it wasn't a full-blown emergency. "Excuse me." I dig out my phone. It's a message from Aleks. *No one's seen the sister. Should I take it outside?* We've made more than one useful contact in the outside world, people with various levels of knowledge about our situation. Bankers to handle our money. Investment advisors to make the most of it. A couple contacts within law enforcement who've been very helpful on occasion. And as much as I want Ember to find her mate, I have all the time in the world to convince her—whereas her sister, also a marked soul mate, is in danger some-where. And that lights up the protective instincts of the entire lair. *Come to my apartment and wait outside the door for me,* I text back.

"Everything okay?" Ember asks, the shock momentarily banished. I'm sure she'll remember later to be outraged about my suggestion that she share deep, soulful kisses with dozens of men she doesn't know, hoping one might be bound to her forever. And she still doesn't understand it all.

I stow my phone. "Aleks says no one's seen your sister. What's her name?"

Her shoulders drop. "Cinder Dubois."

Ember. Cinder. It doesn't escape me the fiery names their parents gave them. I'm sure they had no idea, but the dragon spirit can be strong, even in the womb.

"Have you filed a missing person's report?" I assume she has gotten nowhere with that or she wouldn't have been in my office, taking matters into her own hands.

"She's only been gone for two days." She grimaces, which I don't quite understand. "There's no sign of foul play. The police took the report, but they said she could have just left town for the weekend. I'm pretty sure they filed it in the trash can." She sighs. "I was just sure she'd come *here.*"

"That's a start." I beckon her toward the front. "I'm going to see what we can do to track her down." Her eyes light up with hope. "No promises," I say quickly, "but I've got a few favors I can pull in. Meanwhile, you need some time to, well, think about things. I know this is all really sudden. But I don't want you leaving the castle, just for your own safety. You've got forty dragons here who would give their lives to protect you. It's literally the safest place on the planet for you right now. Just in case whatever happened to your sister comes looking for you."

She frowns but follows me to the door. "You think I'm in danger."

"I honestly don't know what to think." And it's the truth. "I've never had a marked Dragon Spirit walk into my lair before." I give her a small smile.

"Yeah, I'm still not so sure about that." She's wrinkling her nose at me again.

"I know." I open the door, and Aleks is waiting outside. He snaps to attention and stuffs his phone away. "Aleks, find a room for Ms. Dubois. And I want two dragons guarding the door, all night. She might need some food and a change of clothes—get her whatever she needs." I lift my eyebrows to her. "I'll let you know as soon as I find anything about your sister. Acceptable?"

"I suppose." She grimaces. "Yes. Thank you for your help."

"We *will* find her," I vow again. And that's a promise I can easily make. *Two* Dragon Spirits might be enough to keep my lair going for a few more years. Enough to keep the despair at bay.

She nods.

"Do you like balconies or swimming pools?" Aleks asks with a too-eager smile. I recognize my stab of jealously even as I plaster an encouraging smile on my face for Ember to go with him.

Ember scowls. "I like any room stocked with a large bottle of vodka."

My smile becomes a real one.

"We can absolutely arrange that." Aleks would arrange to have croissants flown from Paris, a flock of white doves, and a troupe of circus aerialists delivering champagne if she asked.

It physically hurts me to watch her walk away next to another dragon. I am so fucked with this. But that doesn't matter. What matters is that there's real hope for my brother dragons for the first time in forever.

I close the door and focus on how to find a woman who looks just like the one I'm already falling for.

FIVE

Ember

I SLEEP SO HARD MY DROOL IS RUNNING OFF THE pillow and getting the sheets wet.

Ugh. I drag myself out of the infinitely soft bed. The "room" Aleks found for me is more opulent than a presidential suite at a five-star hotel. The bed is huge, with four posts and gauzy white netting. I have *two* balconies—one off the bedroom and another off the sitting room. The jacuzzi in the bathroom is built for a party of four, the wide-screen TV fills an entire wall, and there's a fully-stocked bar tucked in the corner. Once I was alone, I slammed back two shots just to take the edge off an *insane* day. It took two more before I could get my mind to stop racing and finally float into a buzzed-out sleep.

Forty dragons. It's both way too many to kiss and nowhere near enough to rebuild a population. Even at four times that—assuming the other lairs have just as many—that's barely at the minimum number required for a viable society. I did a piece on it once, looking at everything from indigenous tribes, endangered species, Martian colonies, and how many people you would send on an interstellar spaceship. Turns out no one really knows the minimum viable population—estimates range from 100 to 14,000. But there's literally no one who says forty is enough.

And because the dragons can't find their mates, the real number is much smaller.

Nikolais's people are truly dying out.

Once that hit me, I couldn't think about anything else. All this craziness about soul mates and True Kisses fades when I think about these Vardigah trying to exterminate an entire people— and it looks like they'll succeed in the end. Yet Nikolais seems so convinced that I can help save them. Which, yes, I want to but... that means kids. Probably lots of kids. And, I guess, some hot guy who's my "soul mate." But those things weren't part of my plan. I mean, I've had plenty of hot guys in my life. They're fun for a while, and then I get back to the serious work that I do for a living—reporting on the atrocities around the world, especially how women and girls pay the heaviest price, including this trafficking documentary that Cinder and I are working. That we *were* working before I left her alone for ten fatal seconds that knocked the stuffing out of her. Once I find her—I *refuse* to entertain any other option—all my focus has to be on getting my beautiful sister back to the shining spirit she is... not dragging her into this crazy dragon business. But how can I avoid that when Nikolais seems to think we're both key to saving his people?

Fuck. This is so messed up.

I haul myself out of the expansive bed and stumble into the main room. There's breakfast laid out on the table next to the balcony—because I'm apparently some pampered princess now. I sit down and inhale the omelet, croissants, fruit, and juice. When I stop to breathe, I lean back and gaze out at the beauty of the Thousand Islands. I can see why Nikolais chose this place. It's so remote his dragons can stretch their wings without attracting too much notice. And they can circulate a constant stream of visitors for "parties" to at least attempt to find mates. No one within sight on the nearest islands. No neighbors to complain. Do the dragon men really just *kiss* all those women I saw parading through the main hall last night? At least one couple took it further. Does that happen a lot? Does it get old? Does it get *lonely?*

Those questions apply uncomfortably well to my chaotic sex life.

Damn, my mind won't shut off with this.

I drag my ass into the giant stone-and-brass bathroom. There's a neatly folded pile of clothes next to the towels, another gift for the princess. I step into the shower—the head is two feet across and gushes like I'm standing in a downpour. It feels good to just let the water drench me, but eventually, I get busy with cleaning up. The clothes that magically appeared while I slept are extremely well-made. Some designer I vaguely recognize, but it's essentially black pants and a silky white blouse. Even the underwear is fancy. My hair takes forever to dry, so I just towel it off and let it go. In the mirror, I look like a half-drowned socialite who fell in the pool after doing heroin... but it's not drugs, or even shots of vodka, that's put shadows under my eyes.

What the hell do I do?

This isn't a story, that much is clear. It's much bigger. It has the same expansive feel as when I discovered that sex trafficking ring as part of my story on corruption in the NYC government offices. Powerful men trading access to girls—many underage, all abused—as if they were merely *trinkets.* Sex toys for them to use and abuse. Those fucking assholes *destroyed* girls' lives and went right back to their families and powerful jobs like it was nothing. Like they were *entitled* to it. Reporting on that story wasn't enough for me—I had to *do* something. That's when the documentary project was born. With Cinder as my camerawoman, the two of us would do what we did best—tell the story of these girls' lives. We would shine a ten thousand watt spotlight on the whole rancid business. If we did it right, we'd get those girls the help they needed, raise money for relief organizations, and bring the public into the fight. The documentary would essentially crowd-source the detection of trafficking, so everyday people everywhere would learn how to *see* trafficking and stop it. Maybe that would make a difference. Maybe we could rescue these girls and women held like slaves and sold ten times a day to these animals who didn't care who they fucked or what damage it caused.

Animals. Last night I met a man who is literally

an animal, and he's a better human than any of them.

The project was our way—Cinder's and mine—of fighting a terrible wrong.

That's what I do.

I can't just drop all that to go around the world kissing dragon men. And repopulating the dragon race. It's just… crazy. The whole thing is crazy.

A light knock at the door snaps me out of my thoughts. I grab my flats on the way to answer. It's Nikolais, with shadows under his eyes too, like he's been up all night, but his eyes still light up when he sees me.

"I hope I'm not too early." He's dressed in different clothes—not the borrowed stuff from yesterday, so at least he's changed—and he fills out those jeans like they're custom made.

"I just finished breakfast." I gesture to my clothes. "Thanks for all this, by the way."

He smiles. "My pleasure." Then he gets serious. "I'm afraid I have no news yet about your sister. But my contact at the NYPD says she can put out a bulletin and she'll push to open a real investigation, see if they can track exactly where and when she went missing. She says they've got a new AI program that can search surveillance footage and this would be a good test case."

"You have friends in the NYPD?" This seems implausible; not least because the city's six hours away.

He smiles again. "There's a lot about us I'm sure you'd find interesting." He cocks his head. "If you're willing, there's something I'd like to show you."

I want to keep searching for my sister, but I'm fresh out of ideas, and it seems like Nikolais Lord has *many* resources of which I'm not aware. "Sure. Lead the way."

He smiles even wider and ushers me down the hall. "We won't be traveling by dragon this time if that's all right with you." He's too cheeky for this early in the morning.

I glance around. The corridor is empty. I lean closer and whisper, "I thought we weren't supposed to use the d-word out here in public?"

"Everyone's still sleeping," he whispers back.

I lean back. "Not you, though."

His expression loses its humor. "I had a lot on my mind."

"Yeah." I avoid his too-serious examination of my face and lapse into silence again. There's just too much churning around in my head for verbal banter with Mr. Hotness.

He brings me down a back staircase to a large garage at the rear of the castle. There's a fleet of cars, but we take what looks like a luxury golf cart instead. A short ride brings us to a long dock that extends out into the water surrounding the island. This isn't the dock where I arrived yesterday with the rest of the catering company—this is on the other side of the island. Several boats are lined up —a party barge, a sailboat, two yachts—but again we end up in the smallest one, just a modest motor-boat. Soon we're motoring away from the castle, the wind drying my hair as it flaps behind me. I stand next to Nikolais at the steering wheel, absorbing the rhythmic rocking of the boat with my body, and for a moment, I let all the worries float away on the wind. I close my eyes and tip my face up to the sun and just soak in the warmth and the buffeting wind and the smell of clean, living things. There are worse ways to spend your life, living at the top of the world, literally and figuratively, in your opulent castle. A lot of women—specifically the ones I've been filming for my documentary—can barely imagine this kind of life, except as the disposable plaything of the kind of men who live in castles like this. At a minimum, I need to know Nikolais isn't one of *those* before I sign up to help him. Although, to be honest—his help with my sister has already slotted him into the Good Guy category in my head. But I need to be careful.

The motor spools down, and I open my eyes and squint. We've arrived at another island with a castle on it.

"Is this your private retreat?" I ask Nikolais as he pulls up to the dock. I have to shade my eyes against the bright early-morning sun.

"No, this is a separate facility." He's busy with the controls that cut the motor, then he hops out to tie up the boat to the dock cleat.

I gauge the rocking of the boat then climb out. "How many islands to you *own?*"

"A few." He smirks. "Dragons are good with money. And we have a really long investment horizon."

"I guess." I just shake my head and peer up at the castle. It's smaller than the sweeping estate that's the lair's central operation. Or just Nikolais's? It's not clear what the hierarchy is here, but he certainly seems in charge.

We take another fancy electric cart through a winding, tree-lined path to the castle, but this stone structure is more modern-looking and practical, with lots of windows like a hotel. We enter through a plain door at the rear, and the guy stationed inside is *hot*. I'm wondering if hotness is part of the dragon genome. He tips his head to us and buzzes open the double doors just beyond him.

Inside is nothing like I expect. *It's a hospital ward.*

Down the brilliant white-and-blue corridor, at the end, is a nursing station. It's tricked out with all the latest monitoring equipment and staffed with two nurses in scrubs. The corridor is lined with individual medical suites, some with doors open, some closed. A young woman emerges from one, beams a smile at us, then scurries toward the nursing station. She's not dressed in scrubs but has a light-purple smock that looks like a uniform.

Nikolais touches my elbow to pull me to the side of the first room. It's dark, and there's no one inside, but the empty bed is surrounded by medical equipment on poles.

He keeps his voice low. "As you've already noticed, dragons don't age the same as humans. Our natural healing ability keeps us looking fairly youthful throughout our entire lifespan."

"But you do eventually die?" I ask. "Or do

you… get sick?" This is all baffling. And it feels intrusive to ask.

"A little of both." His brow furrows. "I debated whether to bring you here, but I think you should see everything. All of what we are and what we're up against."

"Tell me." I mentally nudge Nikolais a little further into the Good Guy category. I like that he answers my questions and doesn't appear to hold back. I've interviewed a lot of people, and it's easy to tell which ones are keeping secrets versus which ones share with an open heart. He's already revealed what has to be the biggest secret of his life… and here he is showing me the ugly parts. The *hard* parts. That takes courage. Or perhaps desperation.

Nikolais nods like he expects this from me. "Mated dragons live longer. There's a rejuvenation that occurs when you find your soul mate. A healing of body that comes from the healing of soul. The opposite happens if you never find your mate."

"You die if you don't find your mate?" I lean back. That brings a whole new horror to the deal. "Like, how long does that take? I mean, how long can you live without your mate?"

"Oh, quite long." He says it like that's supposed

to reassure me. "I've lasted a couple centuries without mine. But that's near the limit. It varies from dragon to dragon, of course. But eventually, the soul stops waiting and, well…" He frowns. "We call it the *Withering.* It only lasts a few weeks, but once it starts, it's irreversible. Essentially, the body shuts down. The regeneration stops. All those decades catch up in a hurry." He gestures to the row of private rooms that I'm just now realizing are *hospice* not *hospital.* "We continue to research ways to avoid it, but nothing promising so far. We have this facility for their final days. It's close to the lair, so they can accept visitors." He gives me a small smile. "Unmated dragons are all male. But we have some women who volunteer to bring comfort to the dragons here at the end of their lives. Sometimes, it's the dragon they've fallen in love with while mate-seeking. Sometimes, the women just don't want to return to the outside world. The nurses are all professionals, but we're grateful for everything the volunteers do."

I'm not a crier, but I'm having to blink a little too much. "You're saying some women fall in love even if they're not soul mates."

He smiles. "That's how it happens with humans, right?"

"I mean, yes, but——"

"The heart wants what it wants." He shrugs. "It's a risk for the dragon and human both. Pregnancy could be fatal. And what if his soul mate shows up after he's settled into a life with someone who's *not* his other half? Then again, what if you let your one chance at love slip away while waiting for someone who may never come?"

I'm choking up way too much.

He tips his head toward the next door. "Let me introduce you to one of my brothers."

Aw, shit. I nod anyway. Nikolais knocks lightly on the slightly-ajar door, but there's no answer. He beckons me in. The shades are drawn, and the lights are low, but not off. A man lies in the hospital bed, asleep. His cheeks are hollowed out, and there are only a few wisps of hair on his head, but you can tell he was spectacularly handsome once. He doesn't look old, not really——more like a young man stricken by cancer or some other disease that wastes him away.

Nikolais goes around the far side of the bed, then gently takes the man's hand, which is lying limp on top of the brilliantly white sheets. He holds it for a moment, but the man doesn't fully awaken. "Grigore?" Nikolais calls softly. "Grigore, wake up,

I've brought a visitor for you." That rouses him enough to slowly blink open his eyes. He takes a moment to focus on Nikolais, but when he does, a smile stretches his already thin lips.

"Niko," he breathes. "You didn't have to come."

"Of course, I did." Nikolais's smile falters. "We missed you at the party last night."

Grigore smiles more. "Had a date." Then he coughs, but it's so deep, it hardly makes a sound.

Nikolais narrows his eyes. "Better not be with Nurse Simpson again. We don't pay her to tend to your fetishes."

Grigore tries to laugh, but it just seems to wrack his body. Nikolais squeezes his hand and glances at me. He'd better not ask me to say anything because I'm barely holding it together.

He looks back to Grigore. "I have some good news. Last night's party brought us a Dragon Spirit. This is her—her name is Ember."

Grigore slowly, shakily turns his head until he sees me. I smile as brightly as I can because there's no way I can speak. Grigore nods to me and twists back to Nikolais. "Holy shit, she's hot."

Nikolais grins. "I know, right?"

I sort of laugh and choke and cry all at the

same time. I cover my mouth with my hand because I can't figure out what else to do.

"So, you see, there's hope." Nikolais isn't even trying to stop the tears leaking down the side of his face. Grigore nods his agreement, but his eyes close. It's clear we've exhausted him just with this tiny exchange. Nikolais squeezes his hand. "You rest, my friend." Then he straightens, wipes his face, and motions for us to go. I scrub the tears from my eyes on the way out, but there's still a huge lump in my throat. Once we're in the hallway, Nikolais gestures us back toward the entrance. He stops by the empty room again.

"I shouldn't have…" He just shakes his head and gives a tormented look down the hall.

"I'm so sorry." I don't know what else to say.

"No, *I'm* sorry. You didn't need to see that." He gives me a pained look like he thinks he's screwed something up.

"I think maybe I did." Not that it didn't rip out my heart and stomp on it. But seeing hard things is part of what I do. Seeing them and telling the story of them. Only this isn't a story.

He gives me a questioning look.

"How long has he been sick?" I ask.

"Just a couple weeks." Nikolais presses his lips

tight, then says, "Grigore is younger than I am. We didn't expect…" His expression flattens out again as he gazes in the direction of the hallway.

"Did he have someone?" I ask. "I mean, *does* he have someone who loves him?" The man is still alive—I shouldn't be talking about him in the past tense.

Nikolais turns back to me. "He was waiting."

I frown. "Like you."

He nods.

"Surely, in all this time… Nikolais, you're gorgeous and amazing. There must have been someone who's fallen for you…"

That pained smile is back along with a short laugh. "I have to set an example. If I don't wait, no one will. And then we'll be the last of the dragons." He lets out a sigh. "It'll probably happen that way, anyway. Maybe it's a mistake to—" He's cut off by the door behind us swinging open.

A man strides in with a girl in tow. He's tall and so beautiful, I'm sure he's a dragon—only this one wears his hair long and his beard rough. The girl is half his size, short and painfully thin. Her gaze darts between all of us without landing on anything but the floor. The three-quarter length shirt sleeves aren't quite long enough to hide the bruises on her wrists. I know that look—this girl has been trafficked or at least abused. She seems underage, too.

I dash a look of alarm at Nikolais, but he's already frowning. "Constantine, my brother. Who's your friend?"

"She's from the outside," Constantine says, and that has to be code for something because it's kind of a weird thing to say. "I was scouting near the city. Saw her being walked into a motel. I, um, *dispatched* the man who held her. And the one who came for her." Constantine glances at me but then goes quickly back to Nikolais. "She needs a place to stay for a while."

"There's plenty of room in the dormitory." Then Nikolais speaks directly to the girl. "You're safe here. You can stay as long as you need."

She nods in a jittery way, like it's reflexive, but she's not sure what to believe.

"I'll get her settled then check back with you." Constantine gives me another glance but then leads away his charge, down the hallway. I guess that's the way to this dormitory?

Nikolais waits until they're out of earshot, then he leans in and says, "We send out scouts to look for the dragon spirited—or our best guess at who might be, based on noble traits—and invite them to the castle." He peers at me to see what I think of this.

"That girl was trafficked," I say through my teeth.

He lifts an eyebrow and nods. "Sometimes, we stumble upon an operation. We rescue who we can and give them a place to stay, here, separate from the castle. They need time to recover from the trauma, and the last thing they need is a bunch of dragons hulking around. As a rule, I don't let the men reveal themselves to the ones we rescue—these girls and women don't need that complication in their lives. That's why I didn't take too kindly to your earlier accusation."

It takes me a moment to figure out what he means—that I accused him of trafficking my missing sister. "Because you're not trafficking anyone. You're saving them."

"Trying to." But he looks grim like he doesn't think he's doing enough. But he has no freaking idea how unique that makes him.

"My sister and I are working on a documentary. It's about trafficking. We're trying, too."

He gives me an appraising look and a small smile. "I'm not surprised."

But I am. By him. By all of this. I turn to face

him more fully. "You know what's sexier than a man trying to save his people?"

Now he's surprised. "What's that?"

"A man saving people who aren't even his own." Then I reach for him, both hands. I run my fingertips over the light stubble on his cheeks then pull his face down to mine. He's still surprised when my lips mash against his. It's sloppy and awkward for a second, then his hands are around my back, pulling me into his chest, and we finally *connect.* His lips and mine. His tongue seeking mine. We tangle for a second, tasting, then his hands find my face and take possession of it. Tilting me, lifting me, deepening the kiss until he's consuming me—he's kissing me like he's never hungered for someone as much as me, and it's firing every nerve in my body. He walks me back two steps, and suddenly I'm up against the cool wall, his hand cupping the back of my neck, protecting me while owning my mouth with his. Then he reaches down and lifts me—like I'm weightless—and hooks my legs over his hips, pinning me against the wall, legs splayed, mouth wide, kissing me with his entire body. Something opens up inside me. The rest of the world has ceased to exist. There's just his body and mine, his mouth and mine, his fingers digging into my bottom, his rock-hard erection grinding me against the wall.

He breaks for air just as I think I might happily suffocate.

"Oh fuck," he whispers.

"Don't stop." I claw my fingers into his hair, bringing his mouth back to mine.

He groans deep, a rumbling sound that deliciously vibrates me all over. He's back to devouring and grinding, just like I want him to—

Something's buzzing. I only vaguely hear it over his moan. Then it buzzes again, and he must have heard it this time because he pauses in the consumption of my body against the wall.

He pants, hard, then pulls back, unhooking my legs and sliding them to the floor. "We can't..." He's breathless and dazed, looking at me with wild eyes. "We can't just... *Oh, fuck."*

"What?" I demand, but then I realize where the buzzing is coming from: *my pocket.* My body is screaming for more contact with Nikolais, but instead, I fish out my phone and stare.

"It's from Cinder." My mouth hangs open. I fumble the text message open, but it's a video instead. I hastily tap it.

"Ember!" my sister cries out from the phone.

Her face looms, tear-streaked, mascara everywhere, lips cracked and trembling. "Help me. These *creatures* have me. They have pointed ears like——" She sees something off-screen, and the video clip just... stops.

Like my heart. I look up at Niko, and his shock is the same as mine.

Oh, my God.

SIX

Niko

———

Everything changed in that instant.

That moment when my heart opened, and I was swallowed whole by Ember Dubois.

Soul mate.

I've lived with those words my entire life, but they're empty sounds compared to the reality of meeting your other half—raw, pure, hungry. *Complete.* Words are failing me with how desperate I am to have her back in my arms.

I can't stop touching her. Her hand in mine, my hand on her back, her burying her face in my chest with the two sobs she allowed herself before we scrambled to return to the lair. She's frantic, and rightly so—the Vardigah have her sister, and that's lighting up the panic in my brain, too. But all the way back to the lair—in the cart, the boat, up the back stairs—all I can think is how to get my mate in my bed and finish what we started.

Not yet. It makes me growl.

"What?" Ember asks as we hurry through the lair to the main meeting room.

"Just frustrated." My *need* for her is short-circuiting every other rational thought. I should be soothing the terror in my mate's eyes, but all I want is to haul her to my apartment, throw her on my bed, and fuck her until she screams. Again and again. Like a barbarian. Never mind that she's terrified for her sister, that we legitimately need to figure out how the fuck the Vardigah got hold of her, and the small matter that Ember has to actually *love me* for the mating to take hold. None of that matters to the primal dragon that's awoken in my belly. He wants her squirming under him while he claims her with his cock, his mouth, and his… *love.*

Holy magic, I love this woman. I was falling for her *before,* but that kiss tossed me right off the cliff. Yet all the decency in me has evaporated like mist in front of the raging storm of my lust. *What the fuck is wrong with me?*

"Okay, now what?" she asks, breathless. We've reached the meeting room. Aleks is on his way. I have two seconds to speak this unspoken thing between us—because we haven't said a damn thing about it in our frantic scramble to get back.

"We'll find your sister." I take hold of her shoulders because I just can't stop touching her. "But Ember, I'm *on fire* inside. You're my soul mate! It's fucking blowing me apart—"

"I'm sorry, *what?*" She looks at me like I'm insane. "What the hell are you saying?" Her eyes are wild.

It strikes me like an iron pole to the chest. I drop my hold on her and stagger back as if I've been physically struck. "You don't feel it." My voice is a whisper.

"The *kiss?* Fuck! Nikolais! We need to focus. My sister is—"

"Captured. I know." I'm struggling to breathe. She doesn't feel it. *What the fuck does that mean?*

She's still looking at me with something between fear and anger. No... *terror.* That's what it is. And it's overriding anything else at the moment. Maybe she felt the connection between us. Maybe she didn't. But right now, she needs something entirely different from me.

"You're right." I'm still struggling to catch my breath. "We need to focus on your sister right now."

"Yes!" She's frantic. "Oh my God, those fucking *things* have her—the ones hunting your people!"

"Hey." I catch hold of her shoulders. She's *shaking.* "It's okay." I pull her into my chest and wrap my arms around her. "We'll get her back. Safely. And when everyone's safe again, we'll talk about... other things." I swallow. It feels so *right* to have her in my arms. And she's shaking less now. That has to mean something, right? But an idea nibbles at the edge of my brain, and it's giving me chills. Ember is a twin —her sister Cinder has the mark, too. What if that means... something? What if she can't bond the same way? Or what if her Dragon Spirit is split between the two? I can't even conceive of what that would mean, so I shove that thought away. I'm in love with *Ember...* and she needs my full attention right now.

"But *how* are we going to get her back?" Ember's sobbing into my chest, which just rears up the beast again, wanting to drive away those tears with pleasure.

I stuff that away too and focus on her. She wants a plan, and we need a plan, so that's what we'll do. I pull back, holding her by the shoulders again. "We know where the Vardigah are. We know how to get there. It's fucking dangerous, but we've got no lack of dragons who'll lay down their lives for one of the Dragon Spirited."

Remarkably, that calms her a little. "They would do that?" She blinks and pulls back. *"How dangerous?"*

"How dangerous is what?" Aleks asks as he strides into the room.

Having him here makes everything feel stable again. "The Vardigah have Ember's sister."

"What?" He looks rapidly between us. "How?"

Ember fumbles to get out her phone and play the video again.

He gives me an incredulous look. "How did they find her? Was it the mark?"

"I don't know. But I'm not willing to lose a Dragon Spirit to them."

Aleks's eyes narrow. "The mated dragons."

"That's what I was thinking."

"Hold on," Ember says. "What are you talking about?"

I tip my head to Aleks for him to explain. I'm still trying to sort this in my head. Because we haven't tried an assault on the Vardigah since the first time, which was such a disaster and almost wiped out what was left of dragon kind. I can't ask my brother dragons to take on such a mission without leading them myself. But if Ember is truly my soul mate, I can't afford to risk one of our few chances to grow the lair. It's all so messed up and tangled with my own urgent, growling need to claim her, I'm not sure I'm thinking straight on any of it.

Aleks is explaining the details of mating powers to Ember. "So a mated dragon's venom can kill a Vardigah, but that's not the key to this, I don't think. I mean, it will help…" He's throwing me worried glances, probably wondering why I've fallen silent.

"What's the key?" Ember demands.

"Transport." Aleks turns back to her. "Mated dragons can move inter-dimensionally. And they can bring the rest of us to where the Vardigah live."

"Ketu and Renn," I say to him.

"They're the only ones who… you know." Aleks looks pained by it. As am I.

"The only ones who *what?*" Ember's voice hikes up.

"I'll explain," I say to her but turn to Aleks. "Tell them I need to talk to them. You can brief them before I get there. Give them some time to think about it."

He nods quickly and takes off.

Ember watches him go. "I don't understand what's happening." She turns back for explanation, and those curious, intelligent eyes stir the primal beast inside me again. I would have fallen for this woman even if she weren't my soul mate. Which is reassuring in a strange way. Because, despite my dragon's insane lust for her, maybe the mating won't actually work between us. Maybe being a twin will interfere. Even if it worked, the mission is insane.

I take a deep breath before explaining. "We'll need a mated dragon to get to where the Vardigah are holding your sister. They not only can travel through the portal, but they're also attuned to that realm. They'll be able to find her no matter what part of that dimension the Vardigah stashed her in. But it's a dangerous mission, even with surprise on our side."

She's soaking it all in. "So Ketu and Renn are the mated dragons?"

"We have several pairs who have mated over the centuries." Several as in six pairs. Hardly much of a showing. A stronger leader might have found a way to improve those numbers. But I did all that I could. "Ketu and Renn are the oldest. They mated just before the Vardigah destroyed our lairs—they happened to be away, honeymooning you would call it now, when the attack happened. They've passed the time when they can have children. The other pairs are still in their prime—still adding to the lair. Renn had her last child three years ago. She told us her fertility had come to an end. We held a party for them…" I trail off because the full horror of it is sinking in.

"Wait, they have a little kid?" The distress on Ember's face makes me move closer, touching her again, almost involuntarily. "You can't send them on a dangerous mission like this!" she says.

"We can't do it without them." I cup her cheek with my hand, running my thumb across it as if I could brush away her concerns that easily.

"Can you… just send one of them?" She grimaces because even that's a horrible choice.

I shrug with one shoulder. "Doesn't matter. They're mated. If one dies, the other will perish. That's what mating *means*, Ember. They share a soul. They're joined."

"That's crazy." Her face is scrunched up. Does she understand?

"It's how we've lived throughout all the lore. And I know Ketu and Renn—there's no way one would go without the other."

She shakes her head.

"I know you don't want to talk about soul mates," I say, gently cupping her other cheek too. Then I can't help it. I kiss her, tender and fast, just barely brushing lips. I still feel it zing throughout my body. The beast rumbles through my chest. "But you need to know a few things."

"I don't think…" She swallows and whispers, "I don't know if I believe in all this, Niko."

I smile, but it hurts. "I know. But it's real. And I know beyond any doubt you are the only woman I'll ever love."

Her lip trembles, and I wish I didn't have to burden her with knowing this. Not now. Especially since I'm not 100% certain about how being a twin affects things. But it can't be avoided.

She's shaking again. "I don't… I don't know if…"

"Shhh." I run my thumb across her trembling lower lip. "You don't have to know anything. Or say you love me back. None of that matters. Here's what does: You are my soul mate. I will lead this mission—I'm Lord of this Lair, and I'll not send dragons into battle with the destroyers of our people without leading the charge. But if I die, the Dragon Spirit within you will perish. We're not mated, so *you* won't die, my sweet, sexy, fiery little Ember. You'll live out your natural life as a human woman. But the dragon within you will be gone." I grimace because I don't know how bad that could be, not really. I only know one case where an unmated Dragon Spirit's soul mate perished—he died in the attack just before they sealed their mating. She went mad, but I can't be sure that wasn't a broken spirit, not merely a broken heart. I say none of this because it cannot help to know. And besides, this mission is to return her sister to her side. *Her twin.* They must have a special bond—I can see it in the frantic desperation to save her—and maybe that will see her through if losing her Dragon Spirit is terribly hard.

"This is all crazy," she protests, but there are tears in her eyes.

"Perhaps I'll live," I say brightly. "One of us *will* bring your sister back. If I return, then you'll have all the time in the world to turn down my advances."

The tears shine brighter, so I kiss her again. Stronger this time. I can't help the rumble deep in my chest—the beast wants her so badly. But it's not my inner dragon that holds me hostage. It's the desperate way she's pulling me in, running her hands into my hair, and returning this kiss that's growing hotter by the second.

I pull back. "Not too much of that," I tease, already out of breath. "We take this too far, and we'll end up mated before I go. And that is *not* okay. Not at this point." Her tears break loose, so I brush them away. "Come on. Your sister's counting on us."

SEVEN

Ember

MY HEART FEELS ON THE EDGE OF SHATTERING.

It's a *physical* feeling, deep in my chest, a quivering that feels half heart-attack, half panic-attack. Cinder's captured. Niko's in love with me. Some mated dragons I don't know will risk their lives— with a little kid at home!—to save my sister. All because they think she's the key to saving their people.

They don't know how damaged she is—or was. And that was before these creatures kidnapped her. That video and her terrified face are on an endless loop in my head. I'm desperate to save her, but these people? Risking their lives? Cinder can't have the pressure of being their savior on her! If she's not already hopelessly broken, I know my sister—that will be too much for her.

And this is all my fault.

My heart lurches again as Niko knocks on the door of the mated pair we're here to see. It's a painful spasm that makes me fold my shoulders in slightly.

It grabs Niko's attention. "You okay?"

I've never been so stressed in my life. "Yeah, I'm fine." I've been embedded with troops in actual combat that was less panic-inducing than this. But then that would only kill *me*—not the people I love. And somehow that category of people is quickly expanding to include the handsome dragon holding my hand and scowling at me like he doesn't believe a word out of my mouth. "I'll *be* fine," I say. "Later. After we rescue Cinder."

He nods with that.

The door opens. Another Greek-looking beautiful man greets us. He has a few tiny lines at the corners of his eyes, but that's the only thing that seems older than the other gorgeous dragon men that fill the lair.

"Renn is in the main room with Aleks," he says by way of terse introduction. He gives me a small smile.

"This is my soul mate, Ember Dubois," Niko says, casual-like as if it's just a given.

Ketu's eyebrows fly up, and he stumbles to a stop. "Aleks didn't mention—"

"We just found out." Niko's calm pronouncement is sending my heart into convulsions. I smile weakly at Ketu. The man smiles in return then grasps hold of Niko's arm and pulls him into a hug. It's fierce, on both their sides.

"Then this mission just got even more critical." He pulls back, a shine in his eyes. "Have you sealed the mating?"

"No." The catch in Niko's voice almost kills me dead on the spot. We're holding hands, so I just squeeze his because I have no idea what to say.

"Well, then." Ketu's expression falls solemn. "We both have something to come back for."

Niko nods, and that lifts the panic a tiny bit. Maybe this will all be okay. Maybe they'll come back and bring Cinder and then... what? Niko and I can become mated dragons? It would take the pressure off Cinder at least. But half my heart palpitations are the panic that all this is moving too fast, too crazy, and that I have no idea what I'm getting into.

"Come inside." Ketu ushers us away from the door where we stalled out.

In the main room, a beautiful woman—stunning, actually, with long blond hair and Marilyn Monroe curves—is perched on a couch with a little boy in her lap. *He's a baby.* Niko said three years old, and it's not like I hang around babies much, but this kid is *small.* And he's hanging onto his mother's neck, staring up at Aleks, who's hovering nearby, with wide blue eyes.

"So it would be right away…" I hear the woman, Renn, saying before she notices us.

The boy wriggles in her lap and points at me. "Who dat?"

"That's our new friend," Renn murmurs and rises up from the couch, shifting the boy to her hip. His chubby legs dangle as she adjusts him. The boy stuffs his pointing finger in his mouth to chew. He's adorable. Big black lashes, tiny nose, little fingers getting all wet with slobber.

"But who dat?" he repeats, pointing a now-wet finger at me again.

The kid wants specifics.

"This is Ember," his father says, smiling too big because everyone in the room knows this isn't a time for smiling. "Say hello like a polite little dragon, Lukaz."

Lukaz reels his hand back in and ducks his head into the crook of his mother's neck. Probably just shy, but it feels like an indictment. Like he *knows* I'm going to get his parents killed. I try to smile at Renn and Ketu, but it just feels false, so I stop.

"How about you go with Uncle Aleks?" Renn says to her son. "See if he can find some ice cream in the freezer."

Lukaz pops his head back up, eyes alight. Then he flings both arms back over his mom's shoulder, reaching for Aleks. "Ice keem!" he declares.

"You know it." Aleks scoops him out of Renn's arms and swings Lukas up and around so the baby lands on the back of his neck, feet dangling forward. "Let's get your brothers some, too." Only when Aleks troops out of the room with the baby laughing and digging into his hair with pudgy fingers do I notice the other boys. *Three of them.* Like little solemn stair-steps in height, lurking at the edge of the room, near the hallway that must lead to the kitchen. They can't be more than a couple years apart, the youngest only a few years older than the baby. How many children do Renn and Ketu have?

My heart is already breaking at the thought of these boys losing their parents. Either one. But it won't work that way. Niko said that if one dies, the other goes. These boys would all be orphans. I feel a numbness come over my body. This can't happen. It's so wrong it feels like the world should make it impossible.

Renn waits until the boys are well down the hallway with Aleks. "We need to discuss guardians," she says to Ketu. She barely looks at me, and who can blame her? "And *not* your brother. I know what you're thinking, Ketu."

"You'd break his heart," he says, but it's not harsh. Almost teasing. "You know that."

She waves that off. "He's unmated. They need a *mother*." She says this like she's a statue—no emotion. No tears. I don't know how it's possible, but I don't think for a second that it's real. Her heart is already shattered, just like mine's threatening to do.

"Adara just had her baby," Ketu tries.

Niko is staying silent, watching them, letting them work this out. I wish I could melt into the floor. I wish *more* that I could not cause any of this, even tangentially.

Renn shakes her head. "They have their hands full. It needs to be Shujin."

He frowns. "She and Rhox have only had one."

"Yes, exactly. Plus Lukaz and Kashin already play together. They're like brothers." Then she stops, and there's a crack in the façade—a single tear she quickly wipes away. To Niko, she says, "When do we leave?"

"As soon as you're able." The price it costs Niko to say those words shows up as a flinch in his shoulders. And somehow that's just too much. Seeing it breaks something inside me.

I have to stop this.

But Renn's already moving forward. To her mate, she says, "We need some kind of plan of attack. Perhaps your brother would be good for that." She gives him a tiny smile, and Ketu crosses the room and embraces her. Renn kind of melts into him.

I take that moment to grab Niko's hand and haul him to the side of the room. "We need to talk!" I whisper.

He scowls. "About what?" He looks back to Ketu and Renn who are whispering something to each other, Ketu's hands holding her cheeks.

"About *this!*" I splay an open hand toward the

obvious tragedy that's about to unfold. "This is all my fault." Then I march back toward the door, hoping he'll follow.

"*What?*" He's keeping his voice down, and sure enough, he trails after me. Once we reach the front door, out of sight of the main room, he adds, "What are you talking about?"

"It's my fault Cinder's where she is." I cross my arms tight across my chest because it feels like my heart's going to explode.

Niko's expression turns incredulous. "You know how the Vardigah found her?"

"No," I admit, waving that off. "I don't know how any of that works. But it's *my* fault she was in such a bad place. I never should have put her in that situation—"

"*What* situation?" Niko's alarm keeps stepping up. As it should.

"The documentary!" I'm practically shouting, so I lower my voice, glancing toward the main room of the apartment to make sure no one's coming to see what the hell we're arguing about. "I should never have talked her into that. I *knew* she was upset about the stuff we saw overseas. I know how she gets. She's sensitive—way more than I've ever been in my life. She sees things in the world that I never would. It's why she's so good behind the camera. But the world gets inside her head, and it *hurts* her…" Tears are stinging the back of my eyes. "She came home because she couldn't take it anymore. And I pushed her into doing the project. I thought that doing something—making a difference—would help bring her out of that dark place, but it just made it worse. And then that little girl who was killed. Right in front of her. It just… pushed her over the edge. Then she holed up in her apartment and then she *disappeared…*" I'm gasping for breath. My heart is giving me pains so bad, I'm clutching at my chest.

Shock and horror have frozen Nico—he's just staring at me as I rant.

"I don't know…" I gasp through the pain. "I don't know how these creatures found her, but she was damaged and vulnerable because of *me*. And if I know one thing, it's that the vulnerable get caught up in these things, these horrible things…" That was why I thought she'd been trafficked at first. It was like my nightmare coming to life. "This is my fault." I draw in a breath. "And I can't let these people risk their lives to fix it." My shoulders slump. The tears surge now that I'm not fighting them anymore. My heart just throbs with a dull pain, like whatever attack it was having is finally done, now that I've decided this can't happen. I can't let it. Cinder's pain and horror are my fault. But I can't let that spread to anyone else.

Niko's shaking his head. He takes me in his arms and hugs me. I'm not even sure why until he pulls back and wipes the tears from my face. "Bad things happen to everyone, Ember. It could have easily been you the Vardigah found."

"I wish they *had.*" Now the tears are everywhere. I scrunch up my face in a ridiculous attempt to stop them.

"You can't do that." He says it so tenderly, with a soft touch on my cheek.

"Do what?"

"Wish away bad things by punishing yourself." His smile is pained. "Believe me, there were a lot of years when I thought the lair would have been better off if I'd perished in the fire."

"What?" I swipe angrily at the tears on my face. "That's crazy."

"So is wishing you were the one taken." His expression is way too kind.

I scowl. "This is different."

"Not really."

I ratchet up to a snarl. "Whatever. The important thing is that I can't let this family get torn apart. Not even to rescue my sister. It has to be me. *I'm* the one who has to fix this."

"And how are you going to do that?" He says it like he thinks I'm confused. Not thinking straight.

But now that I'm not having a heart attack about all this, it's becoming even more clear. My panic, my fear, my desperation—it wasn't all because of Cinder. It wasn't even about Renn and Ketu and all their kids. It was *me* being terrified about what I felt during that kiss—what I knew was true the moment Niko pinned me against that wall with his body and his lust and his love.

He's my soul mate.

And that changes everything. It changes it fast, hard, and completely.

I sniff back my tears and look him dead in the eye. "I'll become a mated dragon."

"What?" It's like the words didn't even make sense to him.

"We'll mate, I'll get all those powers you talked about, then I'll go rescue my sister."

His mouth drops open. "I… *Ember*… that's not how this works!"

Ketu peeks around the corner. "Everything okay in here?" He's understandably concerned.

Niko grits his teeth. "We'll be back."

I lift my eyebrows, too surprised to say anything. Ketu seems at a loss for words as Niko throws open the door. Then he grabs my hand and hauls me out of the apartment.

EIGHT

Niko

___

"WE ARE *NOT* GETTING MATED."

I can't believe I have to say those words. I kept them locked inside all the way back to my apartment until we could be behind closed doors for this. Not in front of Renn and Ketu. Not in the hallways of the lair where anyone can overhear. But the instant I close the door behind Ember, those words come spilling out of my mouth.

"We're staying unmated precisely so *you don't die!*" I'm shouting at her. Which I hate. I cover my face with my hands and tip my head up to the ceiling, eyes closed, drawing on every bit of patience I have. But she's my *soul mate*—I can't help but be crazed about her being in danger. "Ember, you just don't—" When I open my eyes, she's not standing next to me anymore. "Ember?" I call out. Then I stalk out into the main room, hunting for her. She's on the balcony, in the bright noon-time sun. It's startling how little time has passed since she walked into my lair and my life—just last night, I was grappling with her in my office. But time doesn't matter when you know someone is your other half. When the fates throw them into your path, it changes everything.

"Ember." I've stepped up behind her.

She hears me, she's just staring out at the water and the sun sparkling on the waves. "I know you're trying to protect me." She turns to face me. "I know it because I feel it too. You'll have a better chance in this if you have the powers of a mated dragon. And if *I'm* a mated dragon, I can go too. I can *help.*"

"It doesn't work that way," I protest. "In any normal situation, we would have all the time we need. We'd get to know each other better. Renn and Ketu were together for a *month* before they were sure. Well, Ketu was sure at the first kiss, but he was a dragon. He grew up knowing how it worked. Renn was the daughter of a Senator in Athens. She had no idea—he had to break it to her in stages, and even then, he had to win her love. Mating is a fusion of two halves of a soul, but sometimes the soul isn't ready. Sometimes… the Dragon Spirited are just really stubborn. And they don't want anything to do with this life. And now? With our people dying out? I can understand that. This isn't something you can rush, my love." I move closer because her eyes are filling with hope, and I still can't keep myself from touching her. I brush her cheek with the back of my fingers. "You don't even know how much I wish it were different."

"Because you love me," she says, eyes alight.

I laugh a little. "Even before the kiss. You're a dangerous woman, Ember Dubois. Dangerous to my heart." And I kiss her… because I might not have too many more chances. It thrums through me, the mating urge. The dragon rearing up and hungering for her.

She breaks the kiss. "What if I'm ready?" Her amber-green eyes are gazing into mine.

"You just want to—"

She puts a finger to my lips and leans closer to whisper, "What if I love you?"

My heart lurches, and the dragon stirs hard. "You couldn't… you can't just *say* it, Ember." But my heart is thudding painfully. "The mating is a connection. Your love has to be real. And you didn't even feel it when we kissed—

"What if I did?" She's so close, fingertips on my cheek, her words caressing me across the air. "What if I lied because I was so scared… afraid of what it meant. Afraid of how it made me feel. Like now. When my heart is beating so hard, I don't know how I'm still standing."

"Ember." I want this—*her*—so badly. I slip a hand to the back of her neck and take what I want, just for a minute. My lips on hers, hot with need. My tongue plundering her mouth. Then I reach down to her bottom and lift her up, still kissing her as I carry her back inside. I get as far as the nearest couch and lower her down, climbing on top of her and laying her back, her body under mine, her sweet curves exposed my roaming hand.

"I just *want* you so badly," I pant against her neck, where I'm busy consuming her with nipping kisses. My cock is painfully trapped in my jeans. But just as the haze of lust threatens to overwhelm me —she's arching up into me, encouraging me with every point we touch—I regain some sense and pull back. "But this is crazy." I climb off her and stand back, running both hands in my hair. I don't even know if this will work. And if it does, it's irreversible. She doesn't know half of what she needs to make this decision.

She lifts up on her elbows, looking at me over her still prone body. "How can I convince you?"

I rub my hand over my face then reach for her. "Come here." She's up in my arms in an instant. I kiss her quickly, then lead her back to my bedroom. Because she's right. She shouldn't have to convince me to make love to my soul mate—to join with her, even if the danger is there. Who did I think she was? The kind to shy away from danger? She's *Dragon Spirited*—of course, she will run headlong into danger if it's the noble and righteous thing to do. But I can make damn sure she knows what she's getting into before she does.

I bring her to my bed—it's wide and firm with wrought iron posts and a canopy overhead. I've pleasured a lot of women in this bed and used those posts to bind them when that was the game we were playing, but all of that pales compared to the ways I'll pleasure and bind this woman if she takes this leap with me. Not with ropes or cuffs, but with an unbreakable soul bond that will last our entire lives.

A smile plays across her lips as I sit on the bed and pull her into my lap, straddling me and facing me. I push her long dark hair back, my mouth literally aching to taste her again.

But I'm dead serious about this. "Even if you

truly love me, I still don't know if the mating will work."

The playful, excited look fades. "Why?"

"Because you're a twin." The words are thick in my throat. "I've never known a Dragon Spirit to be twinned. Maybe it's weakened or split between you. And the fact that you didn't feel the soul bond when we kissed—"

"I did," she insists and presses her hand to my chest again. "I felt it again, just now."

The awareness of her as my soul mate is so much a part of me already, I scarcely noticed the extra zing when we kissed. "Okay. Let's say it works. Let's say we make love, and our souls fuse. You'll never have another man. No one will satisfy you like I will."

"Arrogant much?" she asks, but it's teasing. Her eyes are on fire with those words.

"That's not what I mean." I'm fighting the tremendous desire to rip off her clothes with my teeth. She's in my bed. She's straddling my body. *She wants this.* But I need to make sure she knows what it means. "You'll have all the powers of a dragon I told you about. But you'll be forever bonded to me. *Forever,* Ember. That's a long time for a mated dragon. That's why my friends and I were out sleeping our way around Europe, fucking anyone who would have us, because we were young and stupid and thought we would get bored and *boring* after we were mated. Having one person for all the rest of our long lives seemed incomprehensible. I was so wrong. I knew that when I returned to the fire. I've known that during centuries of being unable to find my soul mate. And now, here you are, and you have no idea how much I'm burning for you. But you need to understand. This is it. This is forever. And if I, as a stupid young dragon couldn't understand that, how can you as a human who's known about the dragon world for all of two minutes, really comprehend it? How can you understand what sleeping with your dragon soul mate will mean? Especially if by some miracle, you truly love me?" I'm all out of breath, and honestly, out of the will to stop her. She could simply say, "Shut up and fuck me!" and I would. Because that's all the resistance I can manage.

But her expression is serious now. "I think it will mean babies."

"Only if the Vardigah don't kill us."

She narrows her eyes. "I think it will help keep the man I love alive long enough to make some babies."

It affects me more than I thought it would. "Say that again."

"Babies, babies, babies."

The laugh erupts out of me. I grab hold of her hips and rotate to lay her down on the bed, side by side. "Say that you love me." I'm searching her eyes —I want to *see* her while she says it.

She touches her finger to my lips, outlining them with her touch. "I love you so much it scared the hell out of me. I just about had a heart attack."

"You're incredibly romantic." But my own heart is bursting.

She laughs, and it's light—sweet. Like she's accepted this, whatever it will be, and the worries are gone now. I didn't know that was the signal I was waiting for, but when I hear it, I can't hold back. I press her back into the bed, my mouth on hers, my hands skimming her body once again. As I slide my lips to her neck, my hand finds its way up her blouse. I'm calculating the fastest way to get our clothes off.

"I think…" She's panting, and her hands are digging into my shoulders, encouraging me. "I think I'll get to wake up every morning next to the hottest man I've ever met."

It flushes me with pride, but I can't resist

popping my head up. "Aleks is going to be in our bed?"

She growls—which is the sexiest sound I've ever heard—and shoves me over. I fall on my back, grinning, and she goes up on her knees, ripping her shirt off over her head. I take advantage of that pause in the action to unzip and shove off my jeans. It takes way too fucking long, but by the time I have them off, she's completely bare, crawling over the bed to the pillows at the head of the wrought iron frame. I tear off my shirt and go after her, catching her ankles and dragging her down and flipping her onto her back. She giggles, and *holy fuck* she's even more beautiful naked. Full breasts. Curved hips. Toes that look imminently kissable, so I do, making her giggle more.

"Next time, I'm in charge of removing your clothes." I kiss my way up her leg.

"Is that right?"

"I'll make it worth your while."

Her breath hitches as I reach her inner thigh and spread her legs, readying to dive in. Her *Oh, God* and the dig of fingers in my hair as my tongue gets to work flushes raw, electric pleasure through me. And judging by her moans and the writhing under my face, the pleasure is rushing through her as well. She grabs at the comforter, and I have to hold her down as I bring my fingers in on the symphony I'm playing with her sweet, hot spot.

"Oh my *God,*" she squeals. "How do you— *uhnnn…*" She arches up into me, then convulses, crying out my name and a string of curses that make me smile so much I almost lose my rhythm.

Then I feel it hit—the pulse of magic, like a hot flush that runs radially out from my heart. There's an electric pulse in its wake, and I'm suddenly feverish, head to toe, with an insane need to drive my cock into my mate and complete the process. *The mating magic.* It's only half activated, sizzling and electric on every nerve.

"What is *that?*" Ember gasps, sitting up and staring at me between her legs. It's not *me* she's talking about—for her, the magic has to be twice as strong.

"That's your body," I pant. "Turning dragon." I crawl up her sweet curves, feverish skin against silky softness. "And I need to fuck you so hard right now."

"Oh my God yes please now yes." She's babbling as she falls back on the pillows, and I love it.

I brush the hair back from her face—the heat of

the transformation is making every inch of her skin damp. I kiss her deeply, as I ease into position. My cock is aching to be inside her. I reach for her wrist and bring it over her head. "Hold on," I instruct. It takes her a second, but she gets a good hold on the wrought iron railings. I hook my hand under her knees and open her wide. I'm *not* small, and I want nothing but pleasure for this gorgeous woman I love, but the dragon inside me is thrashing and urging me to ravish my mate, claim her hard and long so that she'll forever remember our first mating as it sears everything *dragon* into her.

I nudge her entrance, just barely getting the head in.

She lets go of the railing and clutches at my shoulder. "Oh, yes, Niko! *Ah.*" She looks down, but our bodies are mashed together—she can't see how much of my cock there still is to go. "I knew you were big, but *fuck!*"

I can barely keep from laughing. "Shall we start over?" I pull out and thrust in slowly again, deeper.

"Oh my fucking… *what?* Fuck!" Her legs are curled up around me now, her feet digging into my back. And *damn*, it is tight. "I'm so hot." She wipes her brow, and for a moment, I forget about the insane pleasure of being half inside her.

"You okay?" I check her face. She's so flushed. That doesn't seem right.

"Yes. *Fuck.*" She's back to clawing at me. "I just need you inside me, Niko. *Now.*"

I need it too—I'm desperate for it—so I push in further before pulling out once more and stroking in all the way.

"Oh, my *God!*" She's clinging to me, back arched, head buried in the pillows.

I stay seated, adjusting—her to my length, me to her tightness. But we *fit.* There's a sudden right-ness to it. As if I've worked my whole life just to find a way to be joined to this woman in this bed at this moment. The sizzle of the magic is still everywhere in my body. I can feel the heat of hers radiating like an oven. This is just the beginning of the song of love we'll play with each other's bodies—we need to finish it together.

"My love," I breathe, begging. I need to move.

"Niko," she gasps. *"Please."*

And so I do. I stroke out and in, starting gentle but quickly ramping up to a thrusting so hard it jolts us both. She's grasping onto the head railing again, and my hand is there too, giving leverage to keep pumping. Her eyes are squeezed closed, and she's mumbling her pleasure as her head thrashes. I'm trying to hold back, trying to make it last, but each stroke unleashes more of the insane lust of my inner dragon, driving me on, thrusting harder. I'm rushing toward a peak, but this isn't one I can go to alone.

"Ember," I gasp as I slam her body with mine.

"So close." Her whimper goes straight to my cock. "Sooo close oh my God. Oh, God, Niko, I'm *coming—!"* Her words escalate into screams, and her thrashing turns to bucking. I feel her clench hard on my cock, coming in waves upon waves that push me right over the fucking edge.

"Fuck! *Yes!"* I groan as I come hard, deep inside her. Pure, white-hot pleasure rips through me, and I empty myself. It goes on and on. *Fuck.* I've never come so hard in my life. I can't see straight for a moment.

Then the second wave hits. The magic blasts through me, turning pleasure into near electrocution. It shoots through every part of me, from my cock to my mouth, which is hanging open, to my hand gripping the iron railing. The metal fucking *bends* in my grip, a sudden strength greater than any I've known coursing through me. I release it, so I don't wreck the bed, and I peer down at the incredible woman who just turned me into a mated dragon.

All doubts are gone—*it worked.*

My soul mate. Her expression is gloriously sated. The fever of her transformation has broken, her skin now cool, if damp, to the touch. She's making a small moaning sound punctuated with whimpers as she grinds slightly around my cock, which is still buried deep inside her.

"Oh… fuck…" Her eyes are still closed, and her hands are limp on the pillows by her head.

I lean forward and nibble at her slack lips. "Was it good for you, love?" If her eyes were open, she'd see my ridiculous grin.

"I think you killed me." She draws in a deep breath and lets it out slow. "Yeah. Definitely deceased. Lying in heaven with an enormous cock in me. Shhh. Don't disturb the dead."

I nuzzle her breasts, something I had no time for in the frantic need to possess her. To complete the mating. I still can hardly believe this is real. In all this time of waiting, I'm not sure when I lost hope of ever finding her. I certainly never expected her to come to me as feisty and beautiful and *compli-cated* as she is. I could never have predicted any of this… and it's absolutely perfect. Even the fact that we still have to rescue her sister from the enemy who took everything from me—it's exactly as it should be.

Mated. One soul. Taking on the world, together.

I give a gentle nip to Ember's tightly pointed nipple. The shudder of pleasure through her echoes through my body. *What?* I bite a little harder. The electric pulse of pleasure makes her twitch... and then zings through the base of my cock and straight out the tip.

Holy fuck.

"Niko." Her hands are digging in my hair, eyes still closed.

I knew mated sex was hot—I didn't expect it to be literally magic.

"I'm serious, Niko," she sighs. "You've killed me. There can be no sex greater than what just happened to my body. It's not possible."

A smile she doesn't see slowly spreads across my face. "Would you like to place a wager on that?"

"What?" She squints to peer down at me. "Are you kidding? We have to go. Or something." Her head falls back into the pillows.

"Not yet." Mated dragons usually have a week of isolation. Just them and their bodies and their newly fused soul. It's tradition, but it's also practical

—everything is new and raw, and their bodies need to adjust to their new powers, as well as the fusing of their soul. We don't have the luxury of a week—but we should take at least an hour. Any less is probably dangerous. And this mission we're going on is dangerous enough. Besides, this time might be all we have.

I trace the circle of her nipple with my tongue, eliciting another delightful shiver that echoes through my body. *Holy fuck,* this will be good. Then I lift up to get a better angle for working my beautiful mate's body. My cock deep inside her, already stirring and getting ready for more. My hand drifting down to coax out even more pleasure from her swollen nub. My bite might have to be reserved for those delicious breasts.

"Oh my god," she breathes, her body already squirming and angling for more. "You can't be serious."

I've never been more serious about anything in my life.

NINE

Ember

"YOU DIDN'T TELL ME," ALEKS COMPLAINS. PRETTY bitterly.

"There was no time." Niko is adjusting my tactical gear, so it fits snugly in the front. I'm still tingly from those glorious two hours in bed with the man, but I insisted that we get moving on this mission.

"You had time to tell Ketu." Aleks seems genuinely miffed. And I know Niko feels bad it slipped his mind in all the panic. Discovering I was his soul mate came in the middle of *everything.*

"If it's any consolation," I say, "Niko barely told *me.*" Which is true—he waited until we were back at the lair.

"It is not." Aleks gives me a glare, but it's fake.

Niko just shakes his head at me, like I shouldn't bother. But I can tell they're best of friends—cousin-brothers really. I don't want to come between them.

We're all in the main meeting hall of the lair, suiting up in a ridiculous amount of gear—me, Niko, Aleks, and Constantine, the dragon who brought in the trafficked girl. My education on my new powers has been swift, just because we don't have much time. Dragons are fireproof, but not *magical* fireproof. Which is apparently the kind that burned down Niko's home lair.

"Do we really need the helmets?" I ask, giving the one sitting on the table a skeptical look. Not sure how all my hair will fit—maybe it just hangs out. Constantine's hair is long but only to his shoulders. He can probably tuck it up.

"Yes, you need it." Constantine reaches for my helmet and flips up the visor. "These flame-resistant suits are magically enhanced—but that won't help much if your hair is on fire." He hands it to Niko to give to me.

I guess my hair is going inside *somehow*.

Niko gives it over to me then works on securing the straps on his own magically flame-resistant suit. "There are mics built-in. Keep the visor down."

We'll look like high-tech firefighters as we attempt to infiltrate the Vardigah's realm and rescue my sister. The helmet has a flap in the back that hangs over my neck to protect it, so I loosen the jacket Niko just buttoned up, feed my long hair down my shirt in the back, then slide the helmet over my head. Niko scowls and comes back to tighten up my jacket straps again while I adjust the helmet.

"I'll be fine." I shoo away his hands. He's making me nervous with all the fussing.

Niko grumps at me. "You *won't* be fine if the Vardigah blast us and you're not properly suited."

"Don't argue with his High Lord Nikolais Blackscale," Aleks says, obviously still salty. "He's always right, you know. Comes with the title."

"Blackscale?" I lift an eyebrow to Niko.

Aleks dives right into that. "He hasn't told you his dragon name?"

"*Aleks.*" Niko squints at him.

"Oh, she *definitely* needs to know this." Aleks makes an imperious face, and I'm seriously about to lose it. "You have the privilege of being mated to his High Lord Nikolais Celosia Gaulumer Thulror Blackscale, Lord Protector of the North Lair,

Keeper of the Dragon Tongue, and Son of Pure Fire."

It's all I can do not to giggle. "Really?" I ask Niko.

He rolls his eyes but doesn't deny it. *Oh my God,* I've actually married into royalty. Well, not exactly *married.* Mating is far more permanent. But definitely royalty.

"Yours truly is a mere peasant by comparison," Aleks goes on.

"Oh, for fuck's sake," Niko mutters, slipping on his own helmet now. "Sorry, can't hear you." His visor is totally up.

Constantine gives the whole thing a pinched look like he can't believe we're joking around at a time like this.

"What's *your* dragon name?" I ask Aleks, barely able to contain my grin.

"Alexsandr Drayce Adunur Blackscale, at your service." He bows. "Slightly Useful Squire of the North Lair, Keeper of Lady's Tongues, Son of Barely Lit Coals."

I'm guffawing inside my helmet.

Niko flips down his visor. "Are you done?" His voice is coming through the headset.

"Not even close." But Aleks pulls on his helmet as well.

"Radio check," Constantine says over the headset, just slightly impatient. "Everyone sound off." A round of *heres* is followed by a moment of silence. It's about time to go.

"Hang on," Aleks says. "We need a dragon name for Ember."

"My name is already *Barely Lit Coals,*" I say with a smile.

"I always knew you were one of the people, my Lady." Aleks gives me an elaborate bow in his tactical gear, and I snort loudly through the mic… then I nearly suffocate trying to hold back the laughter, so it doesn't ricochet around through everyone's helmets. Aleks keeps giving me solemn nods and winks, which is making everything impossible.

"If you two are quite done…" But there's a smile on Niko's face, and it lifts my heart. No matter what happens next, I don't want him leaving on bad terms with his best friend.

Niko takes my hand and then gives Aleks a joking punch in the shoulder before he grasps hold of Aleks's hand as well. Constantine stands on the far side of Aleks and links hands with him. It's the lineup we figured would be best given the limitations on teleportation for mated dragons. Technically, they can go anywhere, including crossing over some inter-dimensional portal that apparently exists in Ireland and is the entrance to the Vardigah's realm. The limit is really in the total mass you can move and knowing where you want to move to. If I were better trained—or had been a dragon for more than a few hours—I'd be able to help more. As it is, Niko will have to get us there. The limit in terms of people a mated dragon can transport is about four, besides themselves. But since that's a mass thing, and these dragons are 100% muscle, we're just bringing three, including me. I'm strong, but I don't weigh in like these guys. We're holding hands because there has to be physical proximity or intertwining in order to not lose people in the transport. Niko knows enough about the Vardigah to target their realm and enough about *me* to pinpoint my twin sister's location within the realm. So, he'll get us there. He assures me that I'll be able to transport back home —I just have to focus on the lair, and I'll return.

My job is to get Cinder home.

Aleks and Constantine are there for backup, but Niko and I are the ones with the deadly venom and supercharged dragonfire—neither of which I know how to deploy. I've only shifted into my dragon form once, and it was completely awkward. I'd be more likely to fall on my face than land a bite on one of the Vardigah—frankly, I'd be better off using my newfound dragon strength and some Brazilian Jiu-Jitsu throws. But the plan isn't to fight, other than defensively. This is entirely a rescue operation. We just want everyone back home safe again.

I just pray we're not too late.

Niko counts it down. We practiced before, and I expected the teleportation to feel strange, like squeezing through a wormhole or spinning through a cyclone, but it doesn't *feel* like anything at all. Yet it's disorienting as hell, just like switching scenes in a Virtual Reality headset. One instant you're *here;* the next, you're in a completely different *there.* We go from the expansive, modern-looking meeting room of the North Lair to a cramped cell where the walls are made of light, and the floor seems like glass. In the middle, my sister is strapped to a reclined chair straight out of a nightmare—there are restraints on her arms and legs and several metal appendages sticking out from underneath, like a giant upturned insect caught with its legs in the air. A red-haired woman is bent over her, palm to Cinder's forehead. She whips her head to us, wide-eyed.

Everyone springs into action.

Constantine reaches the red-haired woman first, snatching her hand away from Cinder's head and twirling her around to trap her against his chest. She's *human...* I think? Dressed in a hooded gown that sweeps the floor. She twists to give an amazed look to Constantine, who's dragging her away from the chair.

Aleks and I are working on Cinder's restraints. But my sister is passed out cold. With dark circles under her eyes and dry, cracked lips. What did that woman do?

"Hurry!" Niko's placed himself in front of the one door in the room—I can barely see the outline in the weirdly glowing walls.

I'm trying to work the heavy buckles on her straps, but either they're locked, or something, and these fucking fireproof gloves aren't helping. I could try to teleport her home without undoing the straps —in theory, it might work—but I also might bring the whole chair. Which is too heavy. Maybe. *Fuck.* I don't know enough about how this works.

"Oh, fuck this!" Aleks says over the mic and starts ripping the restraints straight out of the chair.

Brilliant. I do the same, but just as I pull the last one, the door disappears, and a blast of blue fire sends Niko flying toward us. Aleks and I lunge to cover Cinder, but the magical fire just dissipates into nothing before it reaches us. Standing in the doorway is a creature that has to be Vardigah—straggly, receding hair, elongated face, and pointed ears that stick up above his head. The snarl coming out of his mouth sends chills down my back, but he's not looking at me or Aleks or Cinder, or even Niko on the floor—he's focused on Constantine and the red-haired woman. Only Constantine is on the floor now, and the woman is standing tall, hands out. That's when I see the faint shimmer in the air —some kind of shield between us and the Vardigah.

"Got her!" Aleks yells. He's slid his arms under Cinder's limp, but now free, body. *"Ember!"* he cries. I grab hold of Cinder's hand and close my eyes just as the Vardigah raises his hand like he's going to blast us all. I picture Niko's bedroom and wish like hell I was there. I wish and wish and... forget that I need to open my eyes. Cinder's hand jerks out of my grasp as my eyes pop open to see we've transported—Aleks is laying my sister's body on Niko's bed.

"Please be alive. Please be alive." Aleks's mumbled chant is constricting my heart, but she looks no different than before—which is completely unconscious. And like she's been tortured or abused or something. No bruises or marks that I can see, but... I stumble over to check, but Aleks already has his glove off and his fingers to her throat. "I've got a pulse," he says through the mic. My panic subsides long enough to realize Constantine and Niko haven't returned.

"Oh, God, Aleks... where are they?" I squeak out.

"Where are *you?*" Niko's harried voice comes through the headset.

"Niko!" I gush. "Thank God. We're in your bedroom. Me, Aleks, and Cinder."

"*That's* where you came back?" A shaky laugh comes through the headset. "We're back in the meeting room. I've got Constantine. Couldn't grab the witch, though."

"*Witch?*" Aleks looks up.

"Couldn't be anything else," Constantine says roughly.

"How's your sister?" Niko asks.

My heart is still pounding from the drama of the rescue, but it lurches a little when I look at her.

Eyes closed. Hands limp against the bed. Dark circles under her eyes. "Not good," I whisper.

"I'm on my way," Niko says.

I hope there's some kind of dragon healing for whatever those bastards did to my sister.

And the witch too.

TEN

Niko

"ANY CHANGE?" I ASK, HAVING RETURNED WITH coffees for everyone.

Ember accepts her chai latte and holds it with both hands. "She's started mumbling like she's having a bad dream. Aleks is in there." I don't like the stress lines at the corners of her eyes.

"The specialist is on the way," I say, hoping that will reassure her. Our hospice nurses couldn't do much for Cinder. "But it'll be a few hours. She's coming from Buffalo."

Ember nods, sips her latte, and glances at the hallway to my bedroom. We decided not to move her sister until the doctor arrived. And the fact that Cinder hasn't awoken yet means no one's in any rush.

I hand Constantine his coffee—black, no sugar, no cream. "Thanks," he says. "And we need to talk."

I know what about—the witch back in the Vardigah realm—but that'll have to wait. "In a minute."

He nods.

To Ember, I say, "You want to come back?"

She shakes her head, and I don't insist. Seeing her sister in that state, especially when there's nothing she can do—and I suspect she still blames herself for Cinder going missing—is no good for anyone.

"I'll be back." I give her a quick kiss on the cheek, then grab Aleks's and my coffees.

When I reach the bedroom, Aleks is sitting in a chair next to the bed, placing a cool washcloth on Cinder's forehead. I frown—she wasn't feverish half an hour ago.

He sees me then spies the coffees. "One of those for me?"

I hand it to him. "How's she doing?"

She mumbles something, startling me—almost like she was answering me—but then she lapses into a quieter mode. Less thrashing, but her eyes are still moving under her eyelids like she's having a dream. And her breathing is erratic.

Aleks shrugs but looks pained. "I don't know what's going on in her head, but she does *not* like it." He sips his coffee and sets it down.

I glance at the door—Ember's out of hearing range. "Do you think the Vardigah did something to her?"

"I don't know why they had her at all." He takes the washcloth, dips it in a small basin next to the bed, wrings it, then puts it back on her forehead. "I don't know what this is, Niko." He shakes his head. "But I don't like any of it."

"Ember blames herself for Cinder getting captured."

"What? That's crazy."

"That's what I told her." We both watch Cinder's nearly-silent torment for a moment. "I feel like we should wake her. If she's caught in some kind of nightmare…"

But Aleks is shaking his head. "This is something darker than that." He peers up at me. "She was gone, what? Two or three days?"

"I know, it's not very long—"

"That's a fucking eternity." His dark look is the

closest I've seen to *rage* on my kind-hearted friend's face.

I frown at him. "What do you mean?"

"She's Dragon Spirited, right? I can't think of any other reason they would take her. Plus, you know, *the mark*. But here's the thing… I can't think of any reason for them to keep her alive, either. Right? Why keep a dragon's mate alive? Why go to the bother of kidnapping her in the first place? Why not just kill her?" He looks back to her, and there's pain twisting across his face. "They did something to her, all right. Something bad. And it resulted in *this.*" He gestures vaguely to the twitching and tumultuous dream state. "I just don't know why."

"Maybe it was the witch."

Aleks squints his skepticism at that. "She conjured a shield for us."

"Maybe she didn't want to burn."

"Maybe."

Cinder whimpers like she's in pain and thrashes her head, just once. Like she's saying no.

"Fuck those *fucking* pointy-eared *bastards.*" Aleks rubs a hand across his face like he's trying to collect himself. I can barely stand seeing it, either.

Cinder's mumbling starts again. It sounds like

she is saying something. Then she gasps, and suddenly her eyes open! She's casting wildly around, almost like she can't see. "Ju... Ju..." she says, thrashing.

Aleks catches her flailing hand and captures her attention. "It's okay. You're safe. You're okay now."

She shakes her head at him, only seeming to half see him. "Ju... *Julia!*" she gasps out.

"Who's Julia?" Aleks asks me, but I just shrug. I'm not sure she even knows what she's saying, but at least she's *awake.* That's huge. I look to the door, torn between staying and going to get Ember.

"You have... to..." Cinder's grip on Aleks's hand is so strong, she's pulling herself up with it. "You *have* to." She's trying to get up.

"Cinder, no." He's trying to get her to lie back down. "You need to rest."

"No!" She shakes her head, but I can see the energy in her body fading quickly. "You need to save her."

"Who? Julia?" Aleks gives me a bewildered and panicked look.

I feel it too. Because a sudden, terrible thought is ripping through my mind. *What if Cinder's not the only one kidnapped?*

"You have to try," Cinder says, but she's already collapsed back in the bed, eyes closed, energy drained. Just that small attempt at... *something*... wiped her out. She flails, blindly, at Aleks's hand. He catches it and holds it. *"Try,"* she insists.

"I'll try," Aleks says. "I promise." He can't have any idea what he's promising. Maybe it's just a fever dream and means nothing.

But the tormented look on Aleks's face is the same feeling I have squeezing on my chest.

"Stay with her," I say, and he nods, but I don't think I could have wrestled him away from her side.

I head back out to the main room. "About that witch..." I say to Constantine as I stride up to him and Ember both.

Constantine lifts his chin. "I think she's using the Gift."

Ember frowns. "What's the Gift?"

I slip my hand into hers. "The ability to find our soul mates." It's chilling me to the core. What this means—for all of us.

"I thought..." Ember's frown turns into a scowl. "I thought you said all the witches were wiped out. Just like the dragons."

"And yet we're still here." Constantine's flicking

looks between Ember and me like he's not sure how much to say in front of her.

But she needs to know it all. "If there were any survivors," I say to her, "they'd be in hiding, just like we are. That's how we've survived two hundred years. But if the Vardigah found one and captured her…"

Ember's eyes go wide. "They would be able to find the dragons."

"They'd be able to find *you*," Constantine says. "They find the *soul mates* of dragons. The dragons themselves were never hard to find… until we went into hiding." He looks to me. "You think the witch can find us, too?"

"If she could, we'd already be dead." But I frown. Huge parts of this don't make sense. "If she found Cinder and directed the Vardigah to her, then why not Ember?"

Constantine shakes his head. "We only escaped because of her protection. That shield protected all of us. And the witch had to know we were dragon. Only dragons would come after a dragon's mate in the Vardigah realm. So why protect us? Why help us escape?"

I scowl. "And why do that if she helped the

Vardigah capture Cinder in the first place?" But at this point, I know there aren't any answers. None we can figure out until Cinder comes around—for real—and can give us some.

"We have to go after the witch," Constantine insists. "Or move Cinder out of the lair. Probably both. Because if the witch leads the Vardigah here…"

I frown—but he's not wrong. Although, historically, the witches only were wayfinders to *unmated* Dragon Spirits. Ember should be safe. "We'll wait until she's stable," I tell Ember. But I'm already thinking about what that means. Will Ember go with her? We might have to decamp to somewhere far from the rest of the lair until we sort this out.

"And there's one more thing," I say to them both. "I think the Vardigah have captured another mate."

Constantine closes his eyes and tips his head back—like he's already thought this through and that was the worst he'd come up with. I know exactly what he means.

"Are you saying you want to go *back?*" Ember asks, the horror slowly dawning on her face.

"We can't," I say. "Not until we know who we're

going after." Which means waiting for Cinder to get better enough to give us real information.

Ember seems to understand this. She just nods slowly.

"But Constantine's right," I add. "At some point, we have to shut down this witch."

ELEVEN

Ember

"THAT'S A WRAP." I WAVE AT NIKO TO HAVE HIM cut the camera.

Then I turn and offer up a hug to "Sarah"—that's not her real name, but it's the one we're using for the film. "You're amazing. You know that, right?"

"I know you say it a lot." She gives the tiniest of smiles, but it lights up my heart. "I might believe it someday." She shrugs, and that part breaks my heart again. This girl's barely sixteen, and she's been through hell. She was trafficked for six months before Constantine found her being walked into a motel by the man trafficking her for the night. Or more likely, for half an hour. He would have sold

137

her ten times more if he'd had buyers. And there always seem to be buyers.

"Ember's right, you know," Niko pipes up. He's serving as my cameraperson to finish the documentary while Cinder recovers. And she *will* recover. The doctor could find nothing wrong with her—said she just needed to rest. Which isn't true, but Aleks is constantly by her side, keeping an eye on her. It's only been a week, and she's getting a little better each day. I keep telling myself that. A hundred times a day. "I know grown men who couldn't even *talk* about something this hard, much less go on camera with it to help others."

Sarah ducks her head and shrugs again, but I think the praise reaches her. And I know Niko means it—in fact, I wonder if there aren't dragons holding in their trauma for two hundred years. I'd be surprised if there weren't. I'm working with him to get this documentary finally finished because *I* need the distraction of the work, but he's been amazing. Gentle and kind, strong and sexy as hell. I'm a hundred percent convinced I would have fallen hard for him even if our souls weren't literally the broken halves of a single one fated to be together. No… *fated* isn't the right word. Because I've seen the dragons who wither away before they've ever found their mate. They were meant to be together, too... it just never happened. Which is a horrible, terrible tragedy. I give silent thanks to every good thing in the universe that I found Niko before that happened.

I smile brightly for Sarah. "Okay, we're done here. If you'd like, we can go out right now for that ice cream I promised." Niko turns to start tearing down the camera and the lights. We're set up in one of the empty rooms in the dormitory for all the women and girls who find themselves in the orbit of the dragons. They're regular humans who have no special powers--not the soul mates of anyone, at least not a dragon. But they've found a place in their hearts for Niko's endangered people. Or they've found a refuge, like Sarah.

"That's okay." She climbs off the chair where she's been sitting with her legs folded up, telling her horrific story of abuse in that flat, still-little-kid voice that chills me every time. *She's just a kid.* Still. And these men obliterated a part of her soul. I pray that it comes back, but as she shuffles to the door, habitually tugging her sleeves down even though the bruises are now gone... I just don't know. She turns back to me. "I've got a shift down in the hospice."

"You do?" I give Niko a questioning look.

"Hey, I can't say *no* all the time. Have you seen how persistent this girl is?"

She beams a smile at him, and my heart's about to burst. That happens on the regular around my Dragon Lord, so I'm pretty sure I'll survive. Maybe.

"That's great," I say to Sarah. "Raincheck?"

"Raincheck." Her smile goes with her as she strides out the door.

I turn and hug Niko hard from behind as he's packing up the equipment.

"Hello," he says, then sets my sister's camera down to turn and pull me into his arms. "You okay?"

"I want to rip your clothes off."

His laugh rumbles deep and sexy in his chest.

I pull back and peer up at him. "I have talons now, right? Can I shift just enough to shred those designer clothes you're wearing?"

He grins. "I guess we could find out." He plays with my hair. "Probably should teleport back to the bedroom first. You know, rather than making out in the women's dorm. I'm constantly on the other dragons about that. Need to set an example."

"Ah, you're no fun." I give him a playful shove, just enough to work loose of his hold.

"You're the workaholic here, not me." He takes my hands and brings me back, lightly kissing me on the nose. "But your work is amazing. And important. You need to keep doing it, no matter what's going on here at the lair." *Or with your sister.* He doesn't say that part, but I hear it.

"I think Cinder would want me to finish the film." Although I know that was part of what broke her in the first place. And now with whatever the Vardigah have done to her...

"Hey." Niko squeezes my hands. "She *would.* And she's getting better. By the time you've got the editing and post-production done, she'll be ready to watch it with you."

I just nod, then take a deep breath... because that's all I can do right now. "That still leaves time for baby-making." I cuddle up next to his chest.

But his eyebrows lift—we haven't really talked about it. Too busy with all the wild lovemaking to talk about the serious stuff. And I knew babies were part of the deal. "I'm always up for making a baby with you," he says softly. He explained how the dragons are hyper careful about birth control—the last thing they want is to impregnate a human who's not their soul mate. There's a reason that the first time a mated pair have sex the woman gains her dragon powers—otherwise, carrying a dragon baby is all kinds of lethal. So, they make sure everything goes right—find their soul mate, fall in love, everything set—before they risk making a baby. Of course, we risked it on the first try—but we were kind of in a hurry. And possibly dying soon.

I slide my hands into the open collar of his shirt. "Do you think we've already made a little prince?" It's been less than two weeks, but with the time we've spent in Niko's bed, if we were making a human baby, I'd be knocked up already. But for dragons, on top of everything else, Niko says it's hard to get pregnant—and mated pairs usually go through periods of infertility. The female's body has to rest before another baby-making season. But I'm young, and we've just mated, so it should be possible.

His expression softens. "Nothing would make me happier." He cups my cheek and kisses me, then he smiles. "But you know it might take a while. Besides, he wouldn't be a prince. My father and mother were the Lord and Lady Protectors. All the true royalty died in the fire."

I give him a teasing scowl. "Seems like they should have made you king by now. Prince at the least."

"Doesn't work that way." He pulls in a breath. "Besides, you don't earn accolades presiding over the death of your people."

My hand goes instinctively to his cheek. "You're *saving* your people every day."

"With your help, maybe I finally am."

I pull him down into a kiss—a hot and heavy one that says *I love you* and *You're mine* and *I want to make a baby with you right fucking now.* I pull away just enough to whisper, "You need to teleport me to your bed, Lord Protector."

His answering growl and grasping of my rear end have me closing my eyes for the split second it takes for him to take us out of the dorm. When I open my eyes, we're not in his bedroom—*our* bedroom—in his apartment, but at his retreat at the old lair, the one they first came to when the dragons were fleeing their smoldering Athens home.

"I've wanted to have you here since that very first night." His voice is rough as he carries me across the room, toward the canopied bed draped in gauzy coverings.

"I thought you didn't bring women here?" I say between nibbles on his neck, which is exposed by his open collar. I remember him making a point of it on that first night—that he came here for retreats *alone*.

"I was waiting."

"Waiting for what?" Although I think I know.

He pushes us through the drapings and lowers me down to sitting on the edge of the bed. "Waiting for *you.*" The love and lust and excitement in his eyes are setting my body on fire. I need him *touching* me, not *looking* at me. I pull him down for a kiss, urging him into the bed so he'll lay that gorgeous body on top of mine. Now that I'm a dragon, I can take the weight—and the solid press of it sometimes has me nearly coming just from anticipation. But he pulls back. "Turn over," he says. "I need to be inside you right now."

I grin and obey, turning onto my belly with my legs hanging off the bed. But he gives me no time to do anything else—I feel a slight scraping along my hips right before my pants just *fall way.* "What—" My panties go next, and I'm suddenly bare. "Did you just—" Before I can even twist around to look, he's plunging that enormous cock into me. "Oh, *fuck!*" I gasp, clawing at the bed, suddenly filled to the brim and unable to think of anything else.

He grunts as he pulls back and thrusts in again. He's pounding me, *hard,* with an animal passion I haven't seen before, and I fucking *love it.* My sweet, gentle prince—and he is one, if only in his heart—is raging with lust, taking me just as he wants me, in a bed he was saving just for me... I'm wide-mouthed into the comforter, clutching it and panting and bouncing with every thrust.

He groans as the pounding grows stronger. *"Fuck... Ember...* you're so damn hot."

I twist to look back at him, this gorgeous man whose clothes are gone, probably in shreds on the floor, holding my hips with his powerful hands, plunging into me with his cock. The look on his face, as he grits his teeth and squeezes his eyes shut, is the hottest thing I've ever seen.

"I'm all... yours, baby... Forever." My words are broken by the ferocity of his pounding.

"Ahhh!" he says, but it's frustration, not ecstasy. He sinks deep in me, then leans forward, his hand circling around to my front. "Come for me, woman." And with his cock filling me like no other —I've literally had no one close to his size before—his fingers work their magic on my swollen nub.

"Oh, fuck, *yes."* I claw at the comforter anew. Niko's skills in bed are fucking insane. Sometimes I'm practically coming just with the heated looks he gives. Sometimes he torments me with his tongue for an hour before he lets me come. We've already spent a little time in the dungeon, where he strapped me to the edging bench, bringing me right to the brink then backing off, again and again, until I was ready to murder him. But when he finally made me come, it went on for fucking *minutes*. He had to carry me back to our room. But now... now his fingers are working me *hard*, and in no time, I'm screaming and clenching his cock, riding that hot orgasm for all it's worth. It goes on and on, and somehow, having him still and hard and massive inside me just wrenches out every last bit of pleasure.

When the peak finally passes, he pulls out and says, roughly, "On your back, my love."

"What?" I'm literally dazed by the orgasm, it was so intense.

"I want to kiss you while we make a child in your womb." His gravelly voice—*his words*—have me flailing to flip over and give him what he wants. He helps me, grabbing both wrists and hauling me to the head of the bed. There are railings there, just like in our bedroom. And I know by now what he likes, so I grab hold, legs wide for him, back arched in anticipation. He climbs over me until his lips reach mine, his cock poised to take me again. "You complete me, Ember Dubois." His words are hushed, whispered, suddenly formal. I gaze up at him, but he's too close, lips brushing as he speaks. "Your soul is my soul. Your heart beats with mine. You are the greatest treasure I will ever have."

I don't know what to say, but it doesn't matter, because he's sliding inside me once again, long and slow and so filling and complete there are no words necessary. This joining of bodies is the fulfillment of our joining of hearts and literally of souls.

"My love, my love," he whispers as he slides into me again and again, reverent and slow. He's taking his time now, hands skimming my body, mouth plundering mine as his cock fills me again and again. The slow and steady beat of our lovemaking builds and builds the pleasure until it's trilling throughout my body, every part from my toes to my fingers digging into his back vibrating with need. So much need. His ragged breath, the tremble of his lips, tells me he's getting close. He's guiding this, so I hold back. I know what he wants: us both coming together as we make our child. I have no way to know, of course, if *this* will be the time. It might take a hundred more. But this is the first time in *this bed* with his soul mate... and I want it to be as glorious as he's always imagined.

It's so slow in coming that when the peak arrives, it catches me by surprise. Niko's rhythm speeds up. He clutches at my hair, tipping my head back and kissing me. The sudden change in speed and angle has me rocketing to the peak. I cry out into his mouth, back arching into his thrust, my orgasm convulsing around his cock and throughout my body. He groans deep and goes still, buried completely as he gushes his seed inside me. He holds like that, panting and grunting as he comes and comes. When he's emptied himself, we come down together, our bodies molded together on the bed. I've never been so sated, so boneless. So lacking in any desire to move ever again.

He shifts his head to the side to whisper in my ear. "That was fucking insane."

"You're incredibly romantic." My laugh is deep inside and shakes both the bed and us.

He pulls back to give me an amazed look. "Please tell me you enjoyed that."

"Hated every second." I can't contain my grin. "Please do it again."

He smiles, kisses me tenderly, and to my utter amazement, he does exactly that.

Ember and Niko are on their way to their HEA, but will Cinder wake up? And whose mate will she be? Find out in My Dragon Keeper (Broken Souls 2).

Get My Dragon Keeper today!

Subscribe to Alisa's newsletter

for new releases and giveaways

About the Author

Alisa Woods lives in the Midwest with her husband and family, but her heart will always belong to the beaches and mountains where she grew up. She writes sexy paranormal romances about complicated men and the strong women who love them. Her books explore the struggles we all have, where we resist—and succumb to—our most tempting vices as well as our greatest desires. No matter the challenge, Alisa firmly believes that hearts can mend and love will triumph over all.

www.AlisaWoodsAuthor.com

Printed in Poland
by Amazon Fulfillment
Poland Sp. z o.o., Wrocław

49518804R00094